ADVENTURES ON THE ISLE OF MU

Tomorrowverse book 1

Vlad ben Avorham

Copyright © 2017 Vlad ben Avorham

All rights reserved

The characters and events portrayed in this book are fictitious. Any similarity to real persons, living or dead, is coincidental and not intended by the author.

No part of this book may be reproduced, or stored in a retrieval system, or transmitted in any form or by any means, electronic, mechanical, photocopying, recording, or otherwise, without express written permission of the publisher.

ISBN: 9781976784477

Cover design by: Art Painter
Library of Congress Control Number: 2018675309
Printed in the United States of America

CONTENTS

Title Page
Copyright
Opportunity of a Lifetime   1
New Friends and Interesting People   14
Am I really going to do this   30
Surprise! It is a Dinner Party   43
Cinderella   73
Cinderella wakes up the morning after the ball   83
Venture capital MU style   87
Berg's idea of oneness   98
I thought figuring out what fork to use was bad   109
Stutsmann Interview   121
The Wonders of MU   132
How the other half live   145
Unexpected visitor   158
A morning to myself   164
Leaving is harder than expected   178
Epilogue   186
Books By This Author   189

OPPORTUNITY OF A LIFETIME

Seattle Washington May 7th 2025

The email came in just as I uploaded this week's pod cast. I had to read it twice to be sure I read it right. See I'm an independent journalist self publishing my own tech blog. That's what a journalism degree from an ivy league university gets you in the new economy. That and a school loan debt that could have gotten me a house in the suburbs. This might be my break, though. An exclusive one-on-one interview with Michael Shultzinger, yeah that Michael Shultzinger on his new island at that. All I had to do was scrape up the two thousand dollars in airfare or the fifteen hundred in Uber fees to get from Seattle down to LA where he would arrange transport out to his home on MU. Yes that MU the new floating island city state built by him and seven other billionaire tech giants last year. This could take my subscribers from my current measly seven thousand to well over a million with just this story alone. I never thought he would agree to it when I sent the request, especially after I heard he turned down the same offer from MSNBC and the Fox Business Channel. I can't help but wonder what he is thinking, but I dare not think too hard on it as this is my chance to make my future.

I close the email and pull up my bank account. Yeah, talk about disheartening. I can get there, but it leaves nothing to live on and nothing to get back with. My only credit card was maxed out while still at school and the limit wouldn't even cover a week's stay on MU that by all reports is notoriously expensive. Still, this was my one chance. Even if it means being late on the payments, I've got to take it.

I close the online banking app and bring up the Uber website. Saving the five hundred dollars will mean I don't get sleep before the interview, but I'll have a little emergency money if I need it. After 20 minutes of negotiation for the longer than usual trip, my driver is supposed to pick me up in an hour. I spend the time selecting my best suit. It is an older style but still professional enough for the job. Ok just barely, but it really was the best I have. I make sure that it is stored in the cloud so it is accessible from where ever I can find to get it printed. It might cost me an extra fifty dollars for an express print job if I'm running late, but if there are no delays I'll have plenty of time to print it out the less expensive way. Modern 3D printing has made travel so much easier, but it's made the fashions change so rapidly. While if you want open source cloths it's great and cheaper to recycle the material than it used to be to dry clean them. It just isn't appropriate wear for an interview of this nature. I can't afford to download the latest designs, so I'll just have to make do. Can't afford to appear like a small fish, even if that is what I am. Dress for the success you want and all that... No sense dwelling on it now it's almost time for my ride to arrive.

As the Uber driver pulls up, I can't help cringing at the state of his car. This guy might actually be worse off than I am. Still he's clean cut, and while "Jeff" as he makes sure I know, keeps trying to flirt with me, he at least isn't over the top about it. I get in smooth my skirts and pull up Shultzinger's file on my augmented reality glasses. Going over the files on Mr. Shultzinger, it suddenly occurs to me I have no idea what I'm going to ask him.

I mean everyone has seen the interviews about how he built his 3D printing empire, going from his basement in 2018 to completely revolutionizing the manufacturing of everything in 2020. Everyone has hashed and rehashed the anti trust lawsuits that sprang up when he partnered with the largest online retailer and refused to accept any payment but Bitcoin and the resulting cryptocurrency wars that caused the dollar crash of 2021. Directly leading to his formation of the Gang of Eight. Having secured the support of those other top seven Tech Titans, they began work on MU. There was complete chaos when they all renounced American, or in the case of Don MacAllan, British citizenship, and moved on to those decommissioned oil tankers to start construction of MU. Maybe I could ask what he would have used if the advancements in solar tech hadn't cause the oil price to fall enough to put all those tankers on the market so cheap… nah it's a good question but not enough to build a story around. I wonder what Mexico charged them for the use of the Gulf of California to build their first prototype islands… again good question, but it doesn't really cover any new ground. I've got to dig deeper. Maybe if he thinks the MU Sovereign will somehow magically maintain its dominance, or if it will experience the same wild fluctuations that all other national currencies have over the last decade. Valid question… yeah, that's one my viewers will hang on his answer. Still not enough for an entire article, but certainly make a note to ask. I really have to…

"Penny for your thoughts," says a slightly reedy voice from the front seat pulling me out of my musings.

"I'm sorry?" I reply, thinking I may not have heard him correctly.

"I said penny for your thoughts. You seem pretty intent back there, and it's what my mom always used to say when she wanted to start a conversation." He smiled up into the rear-view mirror. "We're going to be hitting our turn for the Loop soon and everything will be on autopilot for the next 350 miles or so. I thought you might like someone to talk to."

I frowned. He was probably just trying to be friendly, but after his earlier flirty comments I just didn't want to deal with it. "I'm working. Sorry, but I really need to get back to it," I said, turning my head away from him even though with the AR glasses it didn't really affect my work space.

"Oh, something I can help with?" he asked not taking the hint.

"Sure if you can tell me the one most important question you would ask someone like Michael Shultzinger or Don MacAllan or someone like that?" it came out a bit more snappish than I would normally have been comfortable with but I was on a deadline and he wasn't helping.

"Oh, if that's all then that is easy-" he started

I couldn't help it, I interrupted angrily. "You think so?"

He laughed easily, "Sure, just ask them what is next."

"What are you talking about? They aren't going to just let slip their newest top secret project, so what's the point?" by this time I was getting really mad and I'm not sure really why.

"Of course they're not going to give out trade secrets or anything, but think about it. When we were kids, I mean I'm 28, so that was probably a little further back for me than for you, but still it was a completely different world. I remember when people still got excited about the newest 'smart phone' as if a phone that barely had a usable AI was smart," he chuckled to himself a bit at some memory or other, "I mean my parents told me that they once camped out for two days to get a new iPhone, now what you print out a new set of AR glasses in two and a half hours and that seems like it takes forever."

Suddenly, it hit me and hit me like a bolt of lightning from a clear sky. He was right, and it was also why I was getting so upset with him. The world is changing so fast and people like the Gang of Eight are the reason. They just invent things that completely upend people's lives and the economy and they don't care. They just move on and invent something new to do it all over again. The real question, the only question that matters is 'what is next'

I let out an audible gasp before I even realized I had, "You're right, you're very right. That is the important question. Thank you. Your off handed comment may have just saved my career." I said still a little shaken by my sudden realization.

"No problem, anything I can do to help a damsel in distress" and he had the nerve to chuckle like he'd said something funny.

Now I am angry again. What a sexist comment, like I need some man to come along and 'save' me. "I need to get back to work, if you'll excuse me". Still angry, I watch him shake his head slightly and heave a nearly inaudible sigh and prepare to take back over from the computer as we drove up on the elevator platform to leave the Loop and go back to the surface again.

It was a quiet ride after that. Oh sure, I felt a little bad about snapping at him but, really this is the 21st century and he shouldn't act like some dark ages brute with his sexist condescension. Irritation freshly kindled, there by driving back any feelings of guilt, I turn back to preparing questions for the interview.

An hour later, I'm leaving Jeff and the awkward Uber ride behind and cautiously making my way to the docks. I hate LA. Oh, it was beautiful; they tell me, 30 years ago but after the depression and the ensuing riots, followed by the quake of 2021, and the ensuing riots, and the social services short fall in late 2021, and the ensuing riots, and the drought, and ensuing water riots this spring, much of the city is still being rebuilt. One time my dad told me about an old movie he watched as a kid called "Escape From LA" and chuckled, saying he never thought at the time how close to right that would end up. Still, it doesn't take long to get past the destruction and the poverty into a gleaming modern port with full facilities.

A quick walk down the pier and, sure enough, tied up at the mooring was a sparkling example of modern decadence. All printed of one piece the gleaming hull shone in the sunlight. It looked like it couldn't wait to jump through the waves. I noticed the name engraved on the bow, "Mara". It was my AI in my glasses that provided the image of a buxom redheaded mermaid draped across the bow like world war two era nose art on an old bomber. The image smiled, waved to me, jiggled almost obscenely, blew me a kiss then appeared to jump into the water. I couldn't help but think that Shultzinger's reputation as a chauvinist and a womanizer appears to be true. Still, he was giving me an opportunity few others ever get... "and why is he doing that again" the little treacherous voice in the back of my mind wouldn't quit asking.

Welcomed aboard by the captain, it was every bit as opulent inside as it was out. I was shown to a small cabin "reserved for my use" as it was put. Everything I could want was laid out for me, including a swimsuit, or I assume that is what it would be, when it grew up and filled out a bit more. Still, I knew I'd be here for at least a three-hour ride and that would give me just enough time for a quick nap, and with luck, enough time to express print my dress and make the interview with a half an hour to spare.

Sleep isn't easy in situations like this, but after half an hour of tossing and turning I finally drifted off.

Stranger in a very strange land

Two hours later I'm on the deck of the Mara watching MU come into view. It's huge. It really is an island. I mean the dimensions are published and everyone has seen the mapping satellite images but seeing it in real life is different. Hard to believe that something twice the size of Central Park in New York, and half as high at the peak as the Empire State Building can really float, but it is.

We sail into the small protected bay designed on the port side of the giant vessel. Past the groomed beaches, and small marinas, on either side and toward the cavernous opening of the commercial port. The stark drop in sunlight as we sail deeper into the docking area makes my eyes useless for several seconds. The captain walks me to the dock he says, "Mr. Shultzinger has arranged everything. Just follow the directions on this pass and you'll find everything you need. Thank you for sailing with us today Ms. Winters". With a formal smile and wave of his hand, I take my first steps onto MU proper. I guess it wouldn't do to say MU's soil, but it sure feels solid. None of the subtle rocking one would expect for something that floats, though I suppose once you get to a certain mass...

Disembarking from the Mara, I find myself being shuffled off to what appears to be a customs station. I look down at the "pass" I was handed and notice it is an active display. I look at it closely and am surprised to see the whole thing is the thickness of the credit card in my wallet. The screen is flashing from blue to white and back to blue again. There was a little red arrow that turned to point at a little kiosk off to the side away from the rest of the crowd. I followed the arrow over and the blinking intensified. As soon as I was within three feet of the kiosk screen, the display sheet in my hand chirped twice and a computer generated young woman's face on the kiosk screen says "Welcome Ms. Winters. As you are an expected guest, please check in at the Guest Offices around the corner, and an attendant there will expedite your way through customs."

The pass is now a solid blue with the port lay out in white on it similar to an old style "blueprint" and a yellow arrow is now showing the path for me to the "Guest Offices". When in Rome, I think to myself as I follow the directions. Inside a rather plain looking unmarked door, there is a rather expensively appointed office and behind the counter is a young man who looks as if he can't be over fifteen. The impression is confirmed as his voice cracks just a bit as he says, "Welcome, Ms. Winters. Will you please come with me and we can get you checked in?"

The young boy smiles pleasantly and his eyes only boggle at me a bit. More cute than predatory, it's hard not to like the eager little puppy. He escorts me through a maze of corridors and finally he knocks politely at one closed office door and waits for the muffled "Yes..." before he opens the door for me and says to the older man sitting behind the desk "Ms. Winters is here. She's Mr. Shultzinger's guest and hasn't been with us before". He smiles at me before closing the door and going back to his spot out in the outer office.

The older bearded man rises politely from behind the desk and with a smile and semi-formal half bow says, "Welcome Ms. Winters. I am Grant Longstrom, head of Guest Relations. Let's see if we can get your paperwork processed and get you through in time for you to freshen up before your interview." he gestured toward the seat on the other side of the desk and waited politely to resume his seat until I had sat.

A bit shocked by the amount they seemed to know about me I couldn't help but ask, "You know about my interview?"

Grant's face broke into a wider grin. "Oh, we know all, see all, tell almost nothing," he says with a mischievous twinkle in his eye. At what had to be my mildly shocked expression, he chuckled a bit and said, "It's not really as mysterious as all of that. Your Pass handed to you by the captain of the Mara has been acting as your ID and a herald for you. Every door you've passed through the AI built into MU has been letting us know how to make your stay the very best. It's how I know you're on a schedule. It's how I know it isn't as tight a schedule as you thought. Mr. Shultzinger has had an emergency come up and asks if it is possible for him to put your meeting off until 1630 hours this evening?" He just looked at me expectantly for an answer.

"Oh, uh I didn't know... Sixteen thirty hours, that's what 4:30PM?" I said, trying to do the math of subtracting 12 hours from the time in my head. They had been electronically tracking me since I got off the boat. 'To make my stay the very best' my sweet ass... I don't really have time to think about that at this point, as he is waiting for an answer. "Um, that means I won't make it back to the mainland in time to fly out tonight..."

Grant just gave a shrug and said, "Mr. Shultzinger has already comped you a three-day stay at the Pagoda, our six star hotel. Unless you have a pressing engagement, he was unaware of he would really appreciate you to stay as his guest. Perhaps it will enable you to send out a more complete segment?"

Again that knowing smile and patient silence demanding an answer. Damn the man thinking he can just re-arrange everyone's schedule to convenience his, but a three-day stay at a six star hotel on MU is a good apology for inconvenience from anyone. "Well, it wasn't what I had planned, but this is a real honor, so of course I can accommodate the new interview time."

"Ah good then. His office has been notified and schedule updated. Now on to our processing procedures. Typically, when a new visitor arrives there is a brief medical screen. For guests, this is completely voluntary. Would you mind submitting a drop of blood for the analyzers? Think of it as a free checkup if you like." He smiled at her. You could tell he really wanted her to go along with this, but she wasn't just going to calmly give up a blood sample to people she didn't know. She didn't think they could discover the family secret from a drop of blood, but you never knew.

"Um, voluntary you say?" she waited and at his nod, continued "I'm not really the volunteering type. Is there anything else you need from me?" She was impressed. The only disappointment he showed was a brief tightening around the eyes.

"A couple of things. First, would you rather have a bracelet or a ring?"

"Um. For what?" I was a bit shocked at how abruptly he switched subjects.

"For your infrastructure access token. Every visitor or guest has an infrastructure access token. It functions as ID and digital wallet as well as a key for your room and any other public building you'll need to access while you stay. They come in a small, tasteful silver ring or a small silver bracelet that you can wear." He smiled and gestured to the wall where a portion of the wall turned to an electronic screen showing the items he described. "Both are water proof and while not indestructible, they are very rugged so they shouldn't get in your way whatever you have planned to do in your free time. If it makes it easier, think of it as a high-tech passport."

I frowned. I couldn't help it. An electronic monitoring system wasn't what I had in mind when I agreed to this trip. "And this is voluntary as well?"

He smiled kindly. "I'm afraid not. This has many reasons. Some are very practical and functional, like the ability to access the infrastructure of MU, and some reasons are security related. This enables us to be certain that people don't overstay their visas or work permits. As a guest, you do not have those same limitations, as your host is vouching for your being here up to his or her 90day maximum, anyway. Still, the ID aspects are the Law."

Grudgingly, I could see his point. Those were valid concerns of a small nation, but I didn't like it. "I suppose it's only for a day or so... I guess I'll take the bracelet."

He smiled warmly and said, "It will be ready for you when you leave. In the meantime, allow me to give you a quick rundown of the basics."

Twenty minutes later, after explaining how to make emergency calls and handle any distress situations. Honestly, it felt more like the safety briefing the flight attendants give before the flight than a customs interview. He asks "Any questions? I've been informed that your Infrastructure Token is ready and your rooms are ready at the Pagoda."

"You say you've been informed, how? You haven't spoken to anyone." This was really confusing me. He spoke several times as if he was communicating with his staff but no one had come in or left the room since I arrived.

He gave a warm rich laugh of genuine pleasure, "Oh that, remember see all, hear all, tell very little... just kidding, let me show you." and with that he stood up and walked back from his chair motioning me to have a seat. As soon as I was settled he said, seemingly to the air, "Ulli, please say hello to Ms. Winters."

I heard in my head, not from an external point, but rather as if it was coming from my head a deep rich male voice with a slight exotic accent "Good morning Ms. Winters, I hope you enjoy your stay with us." I couldn't help it. I jumped out of the chair with a start and must have looked a sight, for Grant seemed genuinely concerned for a moment. "What the hell was that!!"

"It's ok, it's ok, I am so, so sorry. I didn't expect it to come as that much of a shock. That was how I knew when things were ready. Ulli is one of the AI's that control the infrastructure of the island. What you were hearing is a special speaker that is formed into the ceiling. It is ultra sound anywhere but in its directional cone. With in the proper cone, it vibrates the bones of your skull slightly, using your own body as a speaker. They've been around since the late 1990s but never been used much commercially. Here we tend to use them to provide discrete promptings to our staff, so that they all just KNOW what you want when you want it. It's a new level of customer service."

He really looked apologetic over giving me a start, and even though I wanted to be angry, I knew he wasn't intentionally making me look foolish. I couldn't help it. I felt like a back woods savage confronted with an escalator or automatic doors. "I see," I said, feeling damn embarrassed. "I suppose you get so used to it you didn't realize how unexpected it would be."

He nodded, looking a bit shamefaced for causing me the embarrassment. "Just so. MU has been built with many state of the current art features that seemed amazing a year and a half ago, but humans are very adaptable. It's just how things are now. Is there anything else I can do to assist you or are you ready to venture out and explore the wonders of MU for yourself?"

I chuckled a bit, realizing maybe for the first time that this wasn't an interview at a corporate headquarters in America, but really and truly a different country with different laws and customs. "Sorry, it just is really sinking in. This is real. You've really formed a new country. Everyone speaking English and everything, it didn't feel real. I want to thank you for streamlining the customs procedures for me."

He relaxed truly for the first time in the whole interview and a small bit of the formality drained from his face. "You're most certainly welcome. It has been a pleasure to be of service today." With that he walked to the door opening it, just beyond was the young man who had escorted me to this office and in his hand was a small silver bracelet that he shyly fastened on my extended wrist, and what do you know, it fit perfectly.

NEW FRIENDS AND INTERESTING PEOPLE

I walked out of the customs section of the port and into the main public square. People were everywhere, going about their business or playing. There were street performers and musicians in several locations. A large screen at the far end of the cavernous area displayed a clock face, a scrolling stock ticker featuring eight companies in a continuous loop, and the public Wi-Fi code. It really was just like any other large metro area downtown or business district, yet it wasn't. It was on a private floating island in a corporate nation state in international waters in the middle of the Pacific Ocean.

Feeling the need to have some of the familiar once again, I pull out my VR glasses and enter the public Wi-Fi code. Immediately upon the connection, I get a message from Ulli, asking if I would please access the Guest Wi-Fi port instead. Included in the message was a link to sync my IAT (Infrastructure Access Token) with the VR glasses. No sooner had I clicked on the link than the view from my glasses radically changed. Everyone I saw had a small icon above their head. Selecting that icon would give me a small personal profile. Including citizenship, name, contact information, even selected hobbies and interests. Also in the upper left-hand corner of my vision was an icon of a Tiki god mask labeled Ulli, so I activated the icon and a 3D rendered avatar with a frightening Tiki face appeared just to the left of my center of vision.

"Ahh thank you, I can't initiate conversation with guests except in very limited circumstances. After I startled you earlier, I wanted to make it up to you by sort of being your native guide. If you'll have me, that is?" If you've never seen a Tiki god, do puppy dog eyes you are missing out.

I couldn't help it. I laughed out loud and didn't care who saw, "Ok how could I say no to that face." For his benefit, I sub-vocalized. Ulli did a back flip and flames shot up from his head and puffs of steam from where his ears would be.

"Good, let's start with getting you a layout of this place." And immediately a map was floating before my eyes about three quarters transparent so I could see where I was walking, as well as directions of where to go. "So it's three hours before your meeting, shopping, the bar, or up to your suite to freshen up?" He had waggled his wooden eyebrows at the mention of the bar. Who ever programmed him had done an amazing job on his personality matrix.

I couldn't help but giggle at his antics. "The bar can wait. Let's get work out of the way first."

Ulli's avatar gave me a sweeping bow, and the map faded from view and a little flashing arrow appeared, directing me straight to the hotel.

Hotel was a misnomer for the insanely posh surroundings I found myself in. I had to ask Ulli twice if I could afford this. His answer, amusing as always was, "Of course not, but since it's all been comped to you by Mr. Shultzinger, why not enjoy it?" I never really got up the nerve to ask what it actually would cost to stay here. A total of six rooms in this "suite", my own personal pool and four person hot tub, full set of appliances, including some I wasn't completely sure how to use. It reminded me of a movie my grandmother used to watch with me over and over when I was a little girl. A woodsman from the Australian Outback finds himself in an upscale New York City hotel. I'm sort of feeling his culture shock now and it isn't as funny at this end of the joke. Still, with Ulli as my trusty guide I manage to get my 'I mean business' suit uploaded to the printer, at which point I hear Ulli pipe up again, "Oh, come on, LIVE a little. Get a new suit, and just charge it to the room. It'll be ok. I checked you're covered for way more expenses than you'll ever use in a three-day stay. Mr. Shultzinger funded the account with Mrs. Shultzinger's shopping habits in mind." Smoke signals working their way up out of the Tiki's head as he chortled at his joke.

As tempted as I was, I didn't want to start this out with me more in his debt than just for the time he was giving me for the interview. I did upgrade the resolution of the print to give me a more quality suit and I did print out some extra accessories that I hadn't planned on... but open source only. Ulli seemed disappointed somehow. Again, I marveled at how much detail there was in his emotional emulation. It must take an immense amount of processing power to run it this detailed. I'd hate to the be the one paying for the cycles bill on this one. If everyone here had access like this, the processor farm must be just immense.

Still, by 1600 I was as polished up as I was going to get. I was checking myself in the mirror to make sure it was all right, and Ulli let out a wolf whistle. At first I was stunned, but I couldn't help but break out in giggles. His avatar looked like some of those old cartoons they had when my grand Da was little, tongue hanging out eyes eight inches out of their sockets, smoke signals puffing hearts out of the top of the Tiki head. "Stop it!" I scolded, but even I couldn't take myself seriously around the giggles. "Women are not objects to be whistled at you neanderthal! Who programmed you like that anyway?" Shaking my head and feeling guilty for feeling better about myself I started following the little arrow toward my big meeting.

***

I told Ulli to go away until after the meeting. I really couldn't afford a giggling fit if I was to be taken seriously. Who ever programmed that thing needs sensitivity training, but today of all days I needed the tension reliever. Doors just swept open before me as I followed the glowing arrow, and without warning a door opened into the largest "office" I'd ever seen. It was difficult to judge actual space as all four walls, including the door as it closed behind me were view screens projecting a view as if from the absolute top of the island. The floor appeared as if precariously balanced on the peak, gave the unsettling feeling that if you moved too far toward the edge, you could unbalance it and the whole thing would crash. MU was laid out below and blue sky and sea met somewhere off on the indeterminate horizon. Behind the carved teak desk sat the one and only Michael Shultzinger, looking like he just stepped off of a private jet, in a suit that probably was designed just for him and cost more than the house I grew up in. It was all a bit startling. He was facing off to the side with his AR glasses on, talking to someone. He held up a hand, and then quickly ended the call, removing his glasses and rising.

"Ms. Winters, I presume," he said with a cock sure crooked grin and an outstretched hand.

"Mr. Shultzinger, thank you for making the time to speak to me." My voice squeaked. I tried to steady it, but this wasn't a normal situation. His confident almost arrogant manner should be offensive, but when balanced against the easy, almost self-effacing smile that went all the way up to his eyes, it was hard to be offended. This ostentatious display of opulence is obscene, but what do you expect from a man whose net worth is greater than thirty percent of nation states? I shook his hand. It was firm and warm, but like that of a friend, not the usual power play for dominance. Probably doesn't see us mere mortals as a challenge to his dominance. No wonder he married a Ukrainian supermodel and built his own city state. What does he really have to prove?

"Please have a seat. I've blocked out an hour and a half for this meeting." he said with a smile.

Ah, so here's the first power play. He had originally promised me two hours, and he's testing to see if I will complain about being shorted. "I thank you for that. I understand you're a very busy man."

His smile was completely genuine. Seems I had passed some sort of test. Well, two can play at that game. "Since our time is short and I really do want to talk about more important things, I'd like to get some of the 'hard questions' out of the way. My readers and views will expect me to ask." Did he just smirk at me? Damn the man, he did.

Shultzinger waved his hand casually. "By all means, let's get the obligatory out of the way. Life is too short to waste on the predictable."

The arrogance of this man knew no bounds. He's actually looking bored. "First, how do you justify renouncing your citizenship and leaving the country that educated you and gave you the opportunity to become so famously wealthy?" There, let him get out of that.

His eyes rolled ever so slightly, as if the thought of just how skewed the perspective that formed the question was. It wasn't quite as bad as the 'are you still beating your wife', but the entire premise was flawed. Trying not to sigh, he looked her directly in the glasses and spoke for the camera. "I don't. Justify it that is. I can give you reasons if you really want to understand, but as for justifying my actions, that just doesn't happen."

I was a bit taken aback by the intensity of the response. I had hit something here. There was genuine anger underlying his response. Curiously not directed at me personally, but something had him frustrated. Under the arrogance of the statement, there was something else. I couldn't quite place my finger on it. "Ok, not justification then, but help my viewers to understand. The land of your birth is America. America educated you. America provided you with opportunities to become wildly successful, and you have beyond all other men before you. At least in a financial measure, and perhaps beyond that. Why turn your back on America?"

Shultzinger couldn't help it. He did sigh at this point. "Is that how you see it? I suppose it would have to be the view of some. America is the land of my birth, and I loved her very much. The 'education'," the word came out bitterly with noticeable air quotes, "I received actually tried very hard to hold me back. Time was wasted learning about things that have little or no application in the real world and were designed to teach me to be an employee, and unfortunately for jobs that have recently been made redundant and obsolete." He took a deep breath "and as for opportunities, America tried to regulate my business out of business before I had even grown big enough to prove its true potential. Some were concerned with keeping jobs for those who were working in industries that the Additive Manufacturing revolution was automating. Others claimed to be protecting the environment, worried that affordable, quality products available at a whim would overwhelm the landfills. Never once considering the business opportunity provided in reclaiming the raw materials for reuse. Several tens of thousands MU Sovereign a year business, or multimillion dollar if you prefer to use that metric." Lazily waving his hand as if to dispel a foul odor, "It wasn't until I left America that the genuine opportunities were available to me. I'm sorry that it was that way, but sorry doesn't change it."

To say his answer stunned me is an understatement. I'd heard all the libertarian garbage before, but here was an intelligent and successful man who actually BELIEVED it. There wasn't any dissembling about his answers. That was really the way he saw things, right or wrong. It was at least honest. "Uh... Ok, lets try another question then," thinking to move to a less personally sensitive subject, "You mentioned the MU Sovereign, do you think it will continue it's impressive run up or will it level off or even decline as all the other national currencies have?"

Michael leaned back in his chair happy to be back on substantive questions that he wanted to answer for the world. "Well, the MU Sovereign isn't exactly a fiat currency like the other national currencies. The Sovereign is more along the lines of real money than a currency."

I didn't want to interrupt him, but that was too big of a bash against other nation states' money to just let slide by. "One sec, I think I misheard you. You are saying that the MU Sovereign is 'money' but the dollar and the euro and the yuan are somehow inferior?" He actually had the nerve to chuckle.

"Yes, that is true, but I suppose it sounds very arrogant to state it baldly like that, without context as to WHY that is the case."

There he goes again with that crooked smile and a slightly shy look. The man is ANYTHING but shy, so that has to be an act, but it sure seems genuine... "Well yes it does. Care to elaborate? For those of use using the other 'inferior' money?"

Nodding good naturedly, Shultzinger leaned forward and became more animated. "Well, all national currencies at this time are what are known as fiat currencies. They came into existence because a government said you had to use them to settle debts. If you sue someone, in the United States, for example, the winner of the case must accept the judgment in dollars. He can't, for example demand to be paid in diamonds or iron ore or pickled herring." He smiled again at the silliness of his example. "It is why they have 'Legal Tender' laws." He shakes his head a bit as if clearing the cobwebs, "The MU Sovereign is different. No law says you must accept it, nor what its value is, other than it represents the underlying securities that support it. When a company opens on MU, whether a bakery or florist or a 3D printing company," he paused to give her time to understand he meant everyone including himself, "that company submits, along with their charter of incorporation, non-voting preferred stock representing twenty percent of the value of their company. No special deals, no negotiated breaks. Everyone puts twenty percent ownership of their company into the treasury of MU. There are only five hundred million MU Sovereigns in existence. Now or ever will be. So when you accept payment in Sovereigns or hold your savings in Sovereigns, you're actually holding one five hundred millionth of twenty percent of the economy of MU. If it helps to think of it as a share of a mutual fund, that might be a... not perfectly accurate, but reasonable approximation. The net asset value at any given moment is the proportional value of the Sovereigns you hold. A currency is a promise to pay, money is the payment. A dollar or euro or even a bitcoin is a promise of payment, a Sovereign is the payment. Trading value for value, as some have put it. I gave you access to Ulli. Ask him for more details if you're interested. I'm not an economist."

His eyes were alive. He was really passionate about this, to me it all spends the same and I never have enough of it, but I can see his distinction. Try as I might, I can't help but smile as he mentions Ulli. "Yes, I have met Ulli, and whoever designed his personality matrix really had an eye for details." He actually barked a laugh at that.

"Oh, personality matrices aren't programmed so much as grown. Ulli learns from those he interacts with and his personality will grow to fit that individual. I'm afraid out of habit I loaned you my Ulli rather than the generic one most people get, so I hope he hasn't caused you too much distress."

Again shock, "S-s-so when he wolf whistled at me earlier as I was making sure I hadn't put my suit on backwards or anything…" anger was rising in me, and shame at how good it had made me feel. It was once thing when it was just an AI following a program, but this was a totally different situation.

He squinted his eyes shut and suppressed what had to be amusement, though he had the decency to look slightly abashed, "Well, Ulli doesn't have the same social filters as everyone I deal with in daily life, or as I myself exercise. Though if you'll take this in the spirit it is meant, I had much the same reaction when you walked in."

The anger wasn't going away. How dare he? Didn't he know women are more than looks? Was that why I was here? "So, just another pretty face, eh?"

He must have sensed the bitterness in my tone because his entire face clouded over and the storm flashed in his eyes, "Well in part, yes."

This was too much. "What! You admit you only granted me this interview because you liked the way I looked?!"

He shrugged. The bastard had the nerve to shrug as if it was no big deal. "Oh, it wasn't the only reason. Would you like to know exactly how you were selected?"

Rage warred with curiosity. Hell, I'm a reporter, so curiosity won out. "Probably not, but since we've come this far, I might as well know." I sat back steaming and waited for the worst.

With that same frustrated look of arrogant defiance, he started explaining, "Ulli, whom I believe you've met, was tasked with finding the most likely tech blogger to give this interview a fair and honest take. He came up with three. You were in those three. One was a middle-aged man who is fair, but also has had his whole life to make his mark and hasn't, really. One was a very talented young man who had a Mohawk and a bone through his nose. Not the image I want for MU! The third was a talented, and yes beautiful, young woman, who was still trying to build an audience. Who, despite the handicap of an ivy league journalism degree, still managed to fairly report on people. Even those with whom she disagreed. So, given I was going to need to spend an hour and a half of my day with someone, I'd prefer she look like you." he finished, eyes flashing. He really didn't enjoy having his judgment questioned, but no matter how you cut it this was sexist as they come. After a moment's pause to compose his thoughts, he continued, "People are a whole, and not parts. Mr. Bone in the Nose was quite competent, but not professional. Mr. Middle Aged was both competent and professional, but had obviously squandered opportunities in his past to still be where he is at in his career." He let that sink in for a second, then continued "I didn't bring in stupid illiterates either. The genetic lottery affects intelligence as much as appearance. To refuse to consider one but make the other a priority is just politically correct nonsense foisted on us by ugly people who found their way to some power. You'll go far if you can liberate yourself from that thinking and focus on what your potential is as a whole person. I did, when I chose to invest my limited time in you, rather than the equally professional and equally intelligent middle-aged man. I think you have more long-term potential, which is a better investment. I don't do charity, but I do invest in people. It is an investment I expect to receive a return on, in the form of a better world that those people can create. I chose to invest in you, and yes partially because of your age and your appearance. Deal with it."

I was in shock. That had to be the most aggressively given compliment ever in the world's history. Still, it was a compliment and not just on the superficial. This was a very complex man and the interview time would be over well before I could make sense of all of this. Speaking of time, could we really have wasted forty minutes already? "Ok, sexist, but not illogical. I'm not sure if most of the world would see the logic of it redeeming the sexism but we'll let the readers decide. Thank you for explaining it to me as honestly as you have."

He took a deep breath and let it out slowly as the heat faded from his eyes. "See that is what Ulli saw in you, the ability to disagree but remain objective. I'd say there is hope for you yet, but even with my way of looking at the world, that would seem condescending." and he smiled again. A real warm smile with a little trace of the earlier fire, just a tinge of weariness.

"I'd like to think that of myself." This interview hasn't been going as planned and I really need something compelling if I want to prove myself with this... oh go ahead and ask the big question see where it leads. "Well, as you say time is too short for the predictable, so let's ask the only real question that is important. What is next? I don't mean specific projects but rather... I... well as my Uber driver put it, 'they upend the world, and then run off and invent something new to upend it all over again. So tell me what's next?" I tried to smile to take any accusation out of the tone, but don't think I really managed it. This man and his kind had devastated the world economy, upended everyone's expectations of what life would be like and he's not yet even forty, so what else is he going to do?

His eyes lit up and the genuine excitement and energy was back. "Very perceptive, Uber driver. Maybe I should invest in him as well." That crooked grin came back to his face, and he leaned forward across the desk, "Well we've already eliminated homelessness and hunger, at least for any nation that wants to…" I just couldn't let that pass.

"Wait a minute what do you mean for any nation that wants to? Who wouldn't want to do that if they could?"

He shrugged again. "Most of them, apparently. Lets lay out the problem and the solution. It isn't about unavailable resources. Once you have 3D printing and cheap solar energy, food and shelter are no longer an issue of resources. A 500sq ft house can be printed, self-powered mind you, with heat, air, and a water condensing system to pull fresh water right out of the humidity in the air, everything but septic. Even that is possible with a little work, depending on the local regulations… all for what about twenty MU Sovereigns? Ulli, what is that in dollars now?" he stops and you can tell he's listening to the reply, "right about twenty-two thousand US dollars. Far less than the cost of social welfare programs for even one year in the developed world. These are housing units that my company is offering at twenty MU Sovereigns MSRP right now. With the optional aquaponics module, another seven MU Sovereigns, an eighty percent automated system will allow anyone spending just four hours a week to produce fifteen thousand pounds of nutritious fish and vegetables a year, with less square footage than a typical one-car garage. More than enough for the occupants of a 500sq ft house to live on and have surplus as well. These are systems that cost less than one year of welfare programs and have an expected fifty year useful life expectancy. Any developed nation that hasn't eliminated true poverty and hunger doesn't want to." He waited just looking at me as if asking me to dispute it. Problem is I couldn't at least not flat-footed with no research.

So I just nodded a little and said, "I'm sure it is a complex solution. If nothing else, the import fees must be a factor."

He closed his eyes for a moment as if steadying himself, but when he spoke his voice was even and mostly calm. "Exactly. Instead of letting people buy what they want, the government puts a thirty-five percent tax on all products from MU. It's their way of denying me access to their markets since I renounced citizenship and cut them out of their tax revenue. It is the American citizen who suffers."

Again, I couldn't keep quiet. "Can you blame them? When you eight left, there was a noticeable budget shortfall. If you're not going to pay our corporate tax, as all of our companies do, we should at least be able to get something for you to have access to our markets."

He smiled, he genuinely smiled, "Is that what you think happens?"

"Well, that is how the system works..."

"Ahh," he sighed. "Let me let you in on a dirty little secret," he leaned forward conspiratorially. "Corporations don't pay taxes. Oh, they right the checks, but it is the people who buy the products that pay the taxes. Profit margins don't change, only end price. People who want corporations to pay just are hiding the additional tax on the people."

I couldn't argue with him on this because from his way of looking at things I could see his point. "Doesn't really seem very fair to me." I said.

This got a true bark of laughter. "Fair has little to do with taxation. It is why MU runs more on a profit sharing model. Remember when I told you that all companies give twenty percent of their valuation as preferred stock to the treasury of MU?" He waited for my nod. "Well, when dividends are paid out, the MU treasury gets a portion of that dividend. We only collect money when the shareholders get paid. If a company has a poor year, there is no taxation. If a company needs to reinvest in new technology, and no dividend is paid, then there are no funds coming into the treasury from that company. That means that it is in the national government's interest to provide an environment where well-run companies can thrive. We don't choke a few nuggets out of the golden goose, we keep it fat and happy and laying more eggs." He smiled from ear to ear. "Everyone wins."

It couldn't be that easy. Greedy corporations would just lock up the money. "So what happens if no one pays a dividend one year, then what you would do?"

Instead of wiping the grin off of his face like I thought it would, he just grinned even bigger. "Well then, just like all private citizens have to, we belt tighten. In truth, it would be unthinkable for ALL THE companies to not pay a dividend in the same year, but good governments do not view themselves as superior to their people. When the belts need to be tightened they just get tightened all around." He leaned back smugly in his chair as if he had just said a profound thing.

"What about all the poor people who need and depend on the

government?" I asked, thinking of the chaos that would happen if the US government just cut off all spending for a year.

"Oh, that answer is simple. Just don't make them dependent in the first place." Again, he sat there smug and sure of himself.

"Easy to say from your own private island, isn't it?" I didn't want to be insulting, but his statement just didn't reflect the real world. "Isn't that awfully close to 'let them eat cake'?"

He raised an eyebrow. "Let them eat cake, eh? Funny you should mention that." He swiveled the chair and leaned forward again. "A brief history lesson that is rarely ever taught. Yes, she was a brainless twit, but not an uncaring monster. Earlier the King had made a decree that bakers sell cake for the same price as bread, so his subjects could have it too. Price controls like that just meant that bakers didn't bake too much in the way of cake anymore. Why work if you'll lose money, after all? So when she was told that the people had no bread, she said well just let them eat cake instead, after all in her worldview, where a government command could change the laws of economics, cake was the same price. True story but sure isn't taught much in government funded schools, where government as the answer to everything is taught. A class of dependent voter is raised, who will always have no other hope for survival than what government is willing to give them. So they will always vote for the one who promises to give them the most."

That couldn't be what that story was all about. He had to have his facts wrong, but since I couldn't look it up right now, I just let it slide. "Interesting theory," I said.

There goes that damn grin again. "Well, Ms. Winters, I hate to be the one to do this, but Ulli just informed me that our time is up and the Japanese Trade Minister is about six minutes from the door."

NO! this couldn't be happening. He never even got to the big question. I could see my big chance slipping away. "I can't keep Mr. Yammamoto waiting, but I did bring you here on the promise of two hours and you accepted with grace when I had to shorten it. So will you be my guest tonight at dinner? Better interview options there..." There he was, smiling at me again.

"Um... dinner?" all my warning bells were ringing. This man had a reputation for a reason.

"Yes, you do eat dinner?" at my nod he continued "well then join me, and I'll try to put some thought into your Uber driver's very insightful question. Ulli will handle directions. I usually eat late, say around 2000hrs? Excellent, I look forward to it. Mr. Yammamoto is now two minutes out, so if you'll please excuse me?" He phrased it as a question, but the door came open, so I thanked him for his time and passed Mr. Yammamoto in the passageway. It wasn't until I was halfway back to the hotel that I had a realization. I never agreed to dinner, yet I was going to be there. This man was too smooth by half.

AM I REALLY GOING TO DO THIS

This was supposed to be a career making interview. Just because it didn't go the way I had hoped it would is no reason to accept the invitation of a known womanizer to a private dinner. Especially after he admitted my looks were one of the reasons he chose me for the interview. Still, it'll be a public place, yeah right on his own private city state. So what's the worst that can happen? Duh. Put it in check there, Elaine, I think to myself. He's known to be a womanizer not a rapist. Besides, this is Michael Shultzinger, and it isn't like good-looking young billionaires have trouble finding dates. Worst-case scenario, I sleep with him. He can't be worse than Hugo the street artist from last week, and the only thing I can blame that poor life choice on is too much tequila.

"HrrHmm!" At the noise, I jump like someone overheard my thoughts. Feeling a bit like a kid with her hand in the cookie jar, I look around and realize I'm completely turned around and wandering down seemingly endless corridors. "HrrHmm!" I hear again and look around, trying to figure out where it's coming from. Seems like it is everywhere and nowhere and its LOUD, but no one else is seeming to notice. Then I realize. I put on my AR glasses again and there was a flashing light at the bottom of my field of vision. One click and out pops Ulli. "Finally! You are lost, and if you don't let me guide you back to the hotel, you'll never have time to get ready for this evening." He's tapping his foot and looking impatient. I can't help it. I giggle at him. "Well, are you going to ask for directions, or are we going to stand here all day with you laughing at me?"

"Sorry Ulli, why didn't you just say something?" I was so distracted by my own thoughts, now I realize that I have gotten completely turned around.

"My settings won't allow it. You said to leave you alone until after the meeting, but my settings won't allow me to come back on my own without you reactivating me. All I can do is a single sound alarm to remind you to do so." Ulli really looked put out by this. Still, the foot kept tapping…

Finally, I remembered, "Oh, and please help me find my way back to my room. Any idea where we're supposed to go for dinner tonight?"

Ulli did a little dance and shook his head. "It is supposed to be a surprise. The information was uploaded to me but it won't decrypt until thirty minutes before time. I think it is Mike's idea of a joke, though whether on you, or on me I'm not sure. I hate not knowing these things." He really looked put out by it, but walked ahead of me in the corridor like he was stalking prey in the jungle.

"Well, how am I supposed to know what to wear if I don't know where we're going? Answer me that one." I couldn't help smiling at his antics.

"Oh, that's easy. You say, 'Ulli help me pick out the right clothes for dinner.' and I make some inquiries of other Ullies and we'll know the right dress for dinner." He looked at me as if that was an obvious question, "Of course they probably won't be allowed to tell me where but they'll know enough to make sure you're properly dressed for the occasion."

"So you can talk to other Ullies about it? That's actually interesting. How does that work?" I asked as we approached the door to my hotel suite.

"First say the magic words, so I can get started on this project, and I'll explain it all, or at least as much as you like." His hands were gesturing wildly as he ran all around the room, looking behind all the chairs as if there were some great beast hiding there.

"Ok, Ulli find me something to wear to dinner tonight." I smiled at him. I know they are just clever programming, but they really are fun and he certainly helped me regain focus after that disastrous interview.

"See that was easy, now as to how it works. Any Ulli can talk to any other Ulli and we always have to tell the truth up to our privacy settings limits. So If I say to an Ulli help me make sure my human is dressed right for an event, that Ulli will help me do that. If I ask where the event is, his privacy settings probably won't let him answer me. Sometimes we get creative and ask a question that lets us figure it out, and it's funny to watch the human's reactions. If your human gets a secret because of your questions, she's usually very happy with you, but woe unto the Ulli who is on the other end. It's not really the Ulli's fault after all the human sets the privacy settings, but it can be upsetting and no Ulli would ever want to make his human unhappy." the face he made was abject sorrow. He looked as if even imagining making his human unhappy crushed him.

"Well, thank you for explaining that to me. Do I need to review your privacy settings?" thinking maybe I'd overlooked something very important.

"You certainly may at any time but Mr. Shultzinger set mine, and he's very security conscious. He even set it so he couldn't know what I was doing, unless you let me tell him." said Ulli with a very satisfied look on his face.

"So Ullies have to tell the truth but can refuse to answer. Do I understand that right?" I asked as I settled into a large plush leather chair that felt as if it had been built exactly for me, and who knows around here it might have been. The king of 3D manufacturing might print new furniture for each of his guests.

"Quite right. Ullies must tell the truth or not say anything at all. Ullies don't lie, but Ullies are not stoolies." He finished with a note of what sounded like pride in his voice.

I giggled again, and anything that could make me giggle after the way this day was going was amazing. "Ulli did you find out what appropriate attire for this evening is?"

"Already being printed now. You should take a nap. From your physiological readings you haven't been getting enough rest"

"Yes, mother." I said, smiling at him. "Actually, I am tired, and if you have my dress being printed, there is no good reason not to get some shuteye."

As I curled into the most comfortable bed I had ever slept in, I couldn't resist. "Good night Ulli"

The Dress

What is that noise? Groggily, I open one eye and see that the lights are also flashing dimly. I sit up, coming out of one of the best, most restful, dreamless sleeps I've had in years. As I sit up, the lights stop flashing and slowly become brighter and the harsh gong is now silent. I'm just contemplating laying back down when I hear, "Well sleepy head, seems like you needed that." Rolling my eyes, I swing my feet off onto the fur rug on the floor. My feet slightly tickle as they slide into the soft thick pile of the most luxurious flokati rug I've ever seen.

"I'm awake, I'm awake. I'm just not sure how happy I am about it." I grumble, as I slide out of bed and on to my feet.

"Well, let's see what we can do about improving your mood," and the light comes on in the bathroom off main bed room. "I was told to figure at least one hour for you to get ready."

"Told by whom?" wondering who on earth he could have been discussing this with.

"The instruction construct, of course." Ulli said in a tone he might have used if I had asked if water was wet.

"Instruction construct? What is that?"

"The designer sends over with the dress to help you wear it properly. Wouldn't do to have a wardrobe malfunction. At least not an unintentional one, that is." Ulli didn't even seem like he was shocked by his assumption.

"Not unintentional... Oh never mind" by now I was getting used to the fact that this Ulli had some pretty biased views of proper behavior. Then again, I could see a schemer 'arranging' a wardrobe malfunction for Shultzinger's benefit, thinking she might snag him. Nope, it's just that the Ulli was raised by a pig, not in the mood to give Shultzinger the benefit of the doubt, at least not after this 'dinner' stunt of his. Probably some secluded restaurant where no one can see what is happening at the private tables, no doubt. Just what I need, octopus wrestling, while trying to interview him.

"You really should get started. I left an extra ten minutes in the time estimate just to be sure, but some of Dion's creations can be intricate." Ulli said in his mother hen tone.

"Dion? Surely you don't mean a Jean Dion original?" I said, doing the math in my head and coming up with numbers that fit the down payment on a house not the price of a gown.

"Of course. You told me to find out appropriate attire for the location." Ulli said, sounding somewhat unsure of himself.

"Do you know how much Dion Originals COST?" I was almost screaming now as my panic was rising. This dress would be many times over more than my entire wardrobe, and I'm a bit of a clotheshorse. Well, most of us are now that it can all be stored digitally and not take up closet space, as my grandmother would say.

"The funds allotted to the room were quite sufficient. You can talk and shower at the same time. We're down to four extra minutes now." Ulli said again.

"Yeah, yeah, yeah, I'm not like most women. It doesn't take me forever to get ready." I said, as I headed for the bathroom. I looked, and looked again, for the controls but there was just an enclosure with no shower head or faucet handles. "Ulli, how do I work this thing?" I called out as I undressed.

"It is automatic. Just step in and ask for warmer or cooler as you want it," said the voice in my head, not from the other room as I expected. I couldn't help it. I jumped and started to cover up.

"Ulli! I can't shower with you here!" I gasped in shock.

"But I am always here. I was with you every second you slept. How else can I take care of my human unless I am with them?" Ulli sounded concerned, as if afraid he wouldn't be able to do his job.

"I need some privacy. Don't watch." I said, feeling foolish. Ulli was just a program after all, but his wolf whistle from earlier today was still playing through my mind and I couldn't shake it.

"I'm not 'watching' so much as you register on the room's sensors." Ulli said patiently. "It's no different from when you were dressing before the interview."

"Maybe, but I didn't know it then... Oh hell, if this is the worst I have to deal with tonight I should count myself lucky." I said resignedly as I stepped into the shower and as I did, a soft, warm rain fell from the entire roof area. A light fog of a mist came from the walls. The temperature was perfect. Oh, this is what luxury feels like. Suds started forming on my skin all on their own. "Ulli, where is the soap coming from?" I called out.

From a speaker in the other room I hear, "It isn't soap. At least not as you think of it. It is a combination of antibacterial lotion in the mist and the ultra sonic agitators. Better for you than soap and better for the draining apparatus of MU."

I smiled to myself. He was using the speaker in the bedroom to make me feel more comfortable. These Ullies' ability to adapt to their user is simply amazing. Looking down at the mention of a drain, I realized that there wasn't one. The floor just absorbed the water as if it was sinking into the ground. The technology here is beyond anything an average citizen in America will have for probably a decade. It really is just amazing. As I'm standing there just enjoying the feel and musing on the differences when from the other room, I hear again. "Shower time is up and you've used up the whole extra ten minutes I set aside. You really need to start on the instructions to get dressed."

Groaning I step out of the shower, and the suds just vanish leaving only a smooth soft feel to my wet skin. I no sooner realize this than warm air envelops me, drying me and even my hair though it is left a tangled mess.

Dry now, I step back into the bedroom and one wall becomes a view screen and there I am on the other side completely naked but with my body blurred slightly. I'm shocked when the speaker announces, "I am the instruction construct. I will help you properly assemble the custom Jean Dion original for your event this evening." I blink twice, but it seems I am not imagining it. A three-dimensional rendering of me will walk me through this step by step. "First let us work on some grooming. From the box on the dresser you will find the depilatory cream. Any hair you wish removed simply rub the cream over the affected area and then use the towel supplied in the box to wipe it clean. The enzyme will break down the proteins in the hair almost immediately." Then the vid screen faded back to a blank wall. Quickly I do as instructed and wow! It really works. Who would ever use a razor again? I take note of the company's name. If it ever gets FDA approval in the US, I'll buy as much stock as I can afford.

Barely had I finished than the wall returned to a vid screen. "Be certain to wash your hands thoroughly, to avoid any unpleasant complications, and lets start with your hair," Over the next several minutes and three more absolutely amazing products, my hair is now in an elaborate style that looks like a professional spent an hour on it. A girl could get used to this kind of treatment.

"Now you need to retrieve your gown from the replication unit."

Well, time is short, so off I go to the other room and open the lid. There has to be some mistake. "Ulli! We have a problem. Most of the dress is missing! Something went wrong with the printing." The 'dress' if you can call it that, is some completely sheer golden material with only a collection of crystals and what looks like tiny gold nuggets in a swirl around the hem, up over the hips and wispy clouds up to the breasts. Everything else is as see through as pantyhose.

"Well, of course there isn't a problem, that is exactly to the designers' specifications. I double checked it myself." Ulli sounded worried.

I took the box back into the bedroom and found the Instruction Construct on the view screen waiting for me. "Um, I can't wear this." I said. There had to be a mistake. This thing was obscene. Ok, so not obscene, but it was indecent. "Did Michael Shultzinger put you up to this?!?!" I was going from shocked to angry. I'd not be seen in public like this. Ok so maybe I would under different circumstances, but to show up to dinner with him like this would be the same as announcing to the world that I was throwing myself at him to get the interview.

Ulli calls out from the speaker in the main room, "No! I asked Mrs. Shultzinger's Ulli what you should wear to dinner tonight. This is what I was told would be appropriate attire. Do you really not like it?"

"Oh, I like it just fine, but it is totally inappropriate for dinner with a married man! Especially one with HIS reputation!" Still, I was in a bit of shock. Mrs. Shultzinger's Ulli was not what I expected for a source for something like this. "I want you to print me up something new."

"Of course, but there isn't time before we're supposed to be at dinner." Ulli was now truly worried. He knew how important this was to making his human happy and it was obvious to him I was anything but happy with this situation.

"Ok, ok. What about something to cover up with? You know a shawl, or maybe a trench coat or perhaps a burka!" screaming at Ulli wasn't really fair. He did exactly what he told me he was going to do. Still, what kind of message did this send?

"But, but there isn't TIME. You're already five minutes behind on the time expected to get ready! I know this is a big night for you. Mrs. Shultzinger's Ulli let it slip that it was an important evening as well." I suspected by the tone of his voice that if I'd had my AR glasses on he would be pacing and doing back flips by now.

"Very well, I suppose, when in Rome... Just bite the bullet and let's get this done!" No sooner than I had said it than the Instruction construct held up a thin strip of material that looked like plastic wrap.

"We begin with your brassiere. You put it on this way." She mimed pulling one breast toward the center of her body and attaching one end of the clingy plastic on the outside and running it tightly underneath. "It is self adhesive and be sure you pull tight." as she demonstrated pulling the other breast over and adhering it to the underside and up the outside. "This will support without showing and allow for cleavage without being overly restraining, just like so." she said as she finished up.

A second later, I completed the action and to my utter amazement it did feel like I was supported without the normal bound feeling. The dress appeared in her hands and she demonstrated how to securely glue one end just above my hip and then wrap it around twice and over to one shoulder. A couple of dabs of adhesive in strategic places, and the instructions were right. Without choosing to, there would be no unexpected wardrobe failures.

It probably shouldn't be this comfortable to be formal wear, but it seemed to move with me and stretch with me. I could go through just about any normal and natural movement and like magic one of the golden swirls of crystal and beads would cover the essentials while leaving the rest of me essentially bare. Looking in the mirror like this, I couldn't help but be a bit self-conscious, but all modesty aside it looked good on me. Before I could even finish appraising myself, Ulli pipes up from the bedroom speaker this time. "Wow, you look great!"

I couldn't help but giggle. "What no wolf whistle this time?"

With an indignant tone, "Of course not. That would be improper." Then more hesitantly, "Wouldn't it?"

That was it. No mere giggle would suffice. I laughed so hard I felt my eyes tearing up. "Yes, Ulli, that would have been improper."

"Good, I wasn't sure. Your words said one thing, but your body language said another. I wasn't sure what the proper response was." He sounded genuinely relieved.

"Oh, it's alright Ulli, men never do." Shaking my head, I decided to make the best of this situation.

"I must remind you that while my avatar has a male body, I'm not a man. I'm an Ulli. An Ulli's job is to understand. I had thought perhaps my programming was indeed flawed."

"It's ok Ulli, you were the Ulli of a man and one who's a bit of a sexist pig at that. You couldn't help your upbringing." I smiled and reached for the special AR glasses that were printed up to go with this dress and then put on the most comfortable high-heeled sandals I've ever worn. As soon as the glasses were on there stood Ulli doing his happy dance and a back flip just for emphasis.

"We really should be going. I don't want you to be late for dinner." Ulli says as he heads out toward the door in a crouch like he's prowling through the jungle.

"Do we know where we're going yet?" I asked as I followed behind.

"Of course, how else would we get there?" Ulli replied not answering the question.

"Well, are you going to let me in on the secret?" I asked as the door to the hotel room swished closed behind me.

"If you want me to. I am now permitted, though I was told it was to be a surprise." Ulli looked back and a Tiki mask with puppy dog eyes was something that just has to be experienced.

"Oh alright already, lead on." I said with a sigh.

We wound our way through corridors and even into a shuttle of sorts. The trip didn't take more than about ten minutes and I noticed we didn't see another person the whole way. "Ulli? Where is everyone?"

"Oh, they are all here. I just thought you felt uncomfortable being in public in your new dress, so I asked the other Ullies to help me out and clear you a path. So far, we've only really delayed three people and none of them by more than about twenty seconds. Ullies do traffic management well." As he said the last line, he drew himself up to his full height and puffed out his chest with his hands on his hips, doing the superman pose.

I giggled despite myself. He may think he's not a man, but he has their sense of humor down. He would be a charming date, grass skirt and all, if only he was solid. I think I would draw stares dancing with him from those who didn't have permissions to see him. That mental picture sent me back into a torrent of giggles. I need more sleep. I'm getting as silly as Ulli.

SURPRISE! IT IS A DINNER PARTY

I almost stumbled. I stopped so fast. There before me were two large bronze doors with Tiki heads embossed in them. When I say large, I mean at least twelve feet tall and probably six and a half feet wide between them. The Tiki heads had actual flames in them. One was smiling and one was sad. It was comedy and tragedy masks out of flaming Tiki heads. Sensing my cautious approach, the doors automatically swing open. They are at least six inches thick. The things must weigh a ton.

Passing through the doors I'm in an equally grand room, the little entry way screened off from the main room by tropical plants at least ten feet tall and still not halfway to the ceiling. The room beyond the plants looks like a Disney theme park's Polynesian island exhibit, including an honest to god twenty five foot tall volcano with red lighted fountains flowing down like lava and a winding path with foot bridges over the 'lava flows'.

Staring around the room like a tourist at a park, I failed to notice the couple standing by the small gap in the plants, along the only path into the main room. "Ms. Winters, so glad you could make it!" exclaimed a rich voice with a slight Slavic accent. I turned to look and immediately felt a slight pang of jealousy. The tall platinum blonde woman wore her barely there beaded gown with a casual grace and elegance that made me feel like a little girl playing dress up.

I regained control of my facilities just in time to notice Michael Shultzinger standing next to her, looking about as pole axed as I felt. At once his mouth snapped shut, but something must have caused him to strangle slightly because he went straight into a coughing fit. I couldn't help it. I blushed furiously as I realized why he looked like that.

***

Remembering my manners at last, I regained my composure enough to say "Good evening Mrs. Shultzinger. Thank you for your invitation to your amazing home."

Ok, I mostly squeaked it, but she only smiled warmly at me and said, "Please call me Tattianna. Any journalist who my husband respects enough to grant an interview must be an exceptional enough person to make a good friend." The smile wasn't fake or forced. It was as natural to her as breathing. She also seemed to be slightly amused by her husband's condition and his failed attempts to disguise it.

"I would like that very much and please call me Elaine. I would love very much to talk with you as well sometime if are willing? Many of my readers would find you as interesting as your husband, if not more so." I tried to be as sincere as I could, in many ways she was more popular than he was. At least internationally.

"Oh, I'm sure we'll negotiate something," she said with a conspiratorial wink. I was just about to ask her what she meant when I felt the air shift as the doors opened again and new guests appeared. "Please go on in and make yourself at home. We'll join you once we've greeted the last of our guests to arrive."

Just that smoothly, I found myself wandering through the plant wall and into the main hall.

The room was absolutely huge. I mean professional basketball arena huge. There were actual trees growing ten to fifteen feet tall strategically placed around the room and little paths winding their way around them. Along the outer walls there were little grass huts with booth seating in them to provide private conversation nooks, and tables set up at the base of the model volcano. At a rough guess looks to be set up for seating thirty or so guests tonight, but with the room here, they could easily host a couple of hundred without feeling overly crowded.

As I am gawking at the scene, Ulli comes up into my field of vision. "Only you can hear me. If you want to talk to me, you can sub-vocalize as normal or for even more private instructions this little icon," and a small red phone flashed in the lower left of my vision, "will allow you to send me an old-fashioned text message." He used his thumb and little finger to make the shape of a phone and held it to the side of his head. "You can call me anytime." He did a bit more of his normal little Ulli dance and then said, "The globe icon in the upper right of your vision is a map of the public areas of the Shultzinger residence. Open it as you need. Last, I've got a list and bios from the other Ulli in the room and each person you meet will have a name tag above their head and a bio page you can access by giving a slight roll of your head." Ulli wrung his hands a bit. "May I use your bio page off of your website to fill out yours? It really is considered impolite not to have one."

I blinked. I hadn't even thought of that. "Of course, Ulli, thank you." I whispered to him. He went back to his happy dance and seemed pleased. I looked around the room and I was indeed properly attired. All the women had on evening gowns and some of them were, if anything as risque as Tattianna's. I giggled nervously as I realized I had called her that, even if in my own head it just somehow seemed way too familiar, but at the same time she asked and she seemed sincere... It was a bit of a shock to see an elderly lady, Marla Sheldon according to the virtual name tag, making her way among the milling crowd, even her gown was a thin white cotton gauze that made it seem more like she was wearing a cloud than dress. It really made her look majestic. I guess money, and a talented designer, can cover a multitude of physical flaws. The men were all wearing what passed for black tie on MU. It seemed to be an almost casual open jacket and crisp under shirt. There were no ties in evidence.

Even the most severely dressed man at the party had on what looked like US Navy whites with the collar buttoned all the way up, except this was a dark charcoal gray with black accents and a single silver trident shining brightly against the black cloth. He wasn't an overly tall man, not quite six foot, but was at least four feet across at the shoulders. In the meticulously tailored uniform, he gave the impression of a large dark bullet with his barrel chest and bullet shaped bald head. His skin was darker than the usual American black man and closer in complexion to some of the tribes of central Africa. His bald head gleamed in the soft light of the room like patent leather, and his face appeared to be carved of obsidian. Fascinated, I pulled up his bio, Commodore Nigel Whetherby. Retired USN at the rank of Captain, SEAL team commander, multiple decorations and commendations, impressive... Shultzinger's chief of security. Makes me wonder what he really does all day. It's not like Black Beard will probably sweep down on us any time. Must be a pretty cush job for a retired SEAL. He looks up as I am reading the last of the bio and stands a little straighter and manages what appears to be an attempt at a smile (or maybe his onyx face just cracked, and a fractional bow of his head in greeting. Feeling silly to be caught looking, I smile and give a little wave and instead of making it better I just look even sillier, so I hurry off.

Winding my way up the side of the volcano, I take note of the bios of those I see milling below. Chief engineer, Banking executive from Bank of Japan, UN Ambassador from Mexico, three of the Gang of Eight who started this, not exactly the butcher, the baker and the candle-stick maker, more like, lions and tigers and bears oh, my… At this point an attractive young woman in a grass skirt and coconuts offers me a tray filled with various blended drinks with little umbrellas. You only live once, but I make a vow to be very careful with alcohol here. After all, this crowd in its own way is far more dangerous than a bunch of frat boys. After I've made my selection, she smiles and heads off with the tray and I continue my climb still distracted by the bios of my fellow guests.

I reach the top of the volcano and find it a bubbling cauldron of what could easily be taken for lava. If it weren't for three people in full formal wear sitting comfortably in it talking to each other pleasantly. I pull my glasses down a bit to be able to see over them, but the lava doesn't disappear, so this isn't a casual VR illusion. Seeing my confusion, an attractive oriental woman stands up, the lava rolling off her dress and pooling around her waist. She smiles and waves, "Do you like my creation Ms. Winters?"

"This is amazing. How are you doing the illusion? It isn't VR." I can't help but return her smile, as it is infectious, and slightly mischievous.

"Oh, it's not an illusion. This really is a bubbling cauldron of rock. Just at the temperature of a good hot tub. Come on in, it won't stain the dress. Feel it for yourself." She says as she wades casually through toward me with her hand out to assist me in stepping into the eight-foot diameter pool of glowing red.

"Umm... I don't know." I can't help but feel a little awkward. Even if everything is exactly as she says hot tubbing fully dressed, or at least as fully dressed as this dress allows, is not a normal act.

The two gentlemen who are in the tub with her both stand as well. The younger man says, "Please try it. It took me three years to perfect the nano particles that make this possible." He's all smiles and reminds me of a little boy wanting to show off a new toy.

The older of the two men chuckles, "Please, I want one, but if I can't convince my guests it is safe, what good will it do me?"

"Um, ok..." I step down and find there is a ledge running around the rim and in another step, I'm finding the bottom is deeper and I'm standing in about four feet of what appears to be boiling lava yet feels very much like a hot tub only dry. I can't help but shiver at the odd sensation. "How is this possible?"

The young man beams. "It's possible and now easy, but it took forever to get the particles small enough to act like a liquid but not stick to clothes." He picks up a handful of the lava and smears it on his jacket, then casually dusts his jacket and it all falls away. "The secret is the polymer chains and the nano-size of each of the grains. You see..."

The pretty oriental woman puts her hand on his arm to stop what she seemed to realize was going to be a very detailed technical lecture. "Tom, Ms. Winters isn't wanting a technical manual." She leans over and kisses him gently on the cheek to take the sting out of her words. "The particles of 'nano-sand' for lack of a simpler term flow like a liquid and are moisture absorbing so even in the warmer temps perspiration isn't an issue. As for our clothes, it's too small and smooth to clump up and cling very well, so even casual movement will shake it all loose." She smiled at me also taking pride in his accomplishment. "Tom is the genius behind the science. I just handle the design elements. I convinced him to make it glow red. When I first saw it, it was a dull gray color, and he wanted to use it for a machine lubricant."

Tom pipes up at this point, "It still will be a great lubricant and change the whole dynamics of a machine's usable life. But even I have to admit, Sandy's idea is more fun." He looks over at her, beaming with pride.

"I have to admit it is amazing. I want to get out now just to see how it will not wreck the dress." Smiling, the entire way back to the side but as I climb back up on the rim of the 'crater', just a casual brush here and there returns the dress to pristine condition. "I've never seen anything like this!" I turn to see the trio climbing up out of the crater behind me. Each in turn gives just a little shake and is as clean as when they went in.

The older gentleman just shakes his head, "I haven't either. I'll take it," He turns to Sandy with a wide smile, "We can discuss the details tomorrow afternoon. I want one, but I want it in black to look like a tar pit. Can do?"

Tom looked concerned and almost said something when Sandy's grip on his arm tightened and she smiled big, "Can do!"

With that, the older man started back down the path toward the mingling crowd. I turned to Sandy. "Congratulations, must be nice not to have to ask price."

Sandy and Tom both laughed, "Not with that one." Sandy said. "And Tom, if Mr. Stutsman wants it in black, we'll figure it out. With what I'll get him to pay for it, you'll be funded for your research for the next three years, and by then you can start selling it as lube for your machines if you want to. In the meantime, let me make us some money." She smiled at him, proud of herself and then realizing she was talking money in front of a stranger turned back to me and waved her hand to dismiss it all. "Sorry about that. Tom really is the brains of our operation as long as we keep him in the lab. He just hasn't come to grips yet with using his amazing mind for making a living beyond being an employee of a company. We went freelance when we moved to MU and this is all kind of new to us."

"Oh, I'm visiting from the US and it's all new to me. You have an amazing invention there. How soon before I see your creations on TV and in high end hotels?" I asked curious if they had planned that far ahead.

Both people grimaced. "In the US?" Tom said and looked a little dispirited.

Sandy shook her head. "Have to go through the EPA and the FDA and who knows what other bureaucracy. I doubt we'll even offer it in the US until someone wants it bad enough to go through all the red tape for it." she sighed. "Oh, you might see Tom's lubricant in four or five years, but to use it like this... maybe in ten years?" She shrugged. "I'm thinking we can get a couple more here on MU and maybe as many as a dozen on Atlantis when it's complete. A couple of dozen more on the smaller islands that are being built for individuals. Maybe fifty in all over the next decade until it's got enough demand to overcome the bureaucrats in the US, the EU, and China." Again she just shook her head and shrugged as if to say, 'what can you do'

"I suppose they want to just be sure it's safe," I said, but even I didn't really believe it as I said it.

They both just smiled politely, and we started walking back down the path toward the milling crowd. As we neared the bottom, I got up the courage to ask, "Sooo... You know I am a reporter, so I've got to ask. How much will something like this cost?"

Sandy grinned. "Off the record, as much as the market will bear. If you're asking what I think Mr. Stutsman will pay. Let's just say I'm going to start at two thousand Sovereigns, but expect we'll probably settle around fifteen hundred. For one that doesn't require special R&D, and would fit at a high end hotel say," she made a face as she was doing the math or I suspected as her Ulli was doing it for her, "probably could get down to as low as fifteen or twenty Sovereigns. At least once we get to that point and are doing some quantity of them."

Doing the math in my head, I blurted out before I could stop myself, "Two thousand Sovereigns! Was that Mr. Rockefeller?"

They both grinned at my incredulous look. "It's Mr. Stutsman. You know of Stutsman AI. The man behind technologies like the Ulli. I didn't realize you didn't know who he was."

I was stunned. I hadn't seen his virtual name tag because I was distracted by people sitting in lava, so I fessed up. "No, I didn't know. People sitting in lava kinda took precedent over name tags. I wonder if I can get him to grant me an interview?"

Tom shrugged. "These dinners are good places to ask those kinds of questions. Just catch him after dinner. Oh, and just so you know, David Rosen is here too. You know the economist who designed the sovereigns. He might be another one you want to catch. Though the last interview he did with CNN, he charged them two hundred Sovereigns for." He shook his head as if he couldn't fathom being able to do that.

I smiled. I couldn't help it. This was turning into an amazing experience. "Thank you. I'll have to keep my eyes open. Seems there are all sorts of amazing people you can meet here." as I nodded to him and Sandy intentionally including them in that company. At their embarrassed smiles, I just waved and walked a little farther down a different path heading toward what looked like a cave entrance but had moonlight showing palely through it.

◆ ◆ ◆

I enter the 'cave' entrance and the glass doors retract, letting a cool salt breeze through. The terrace on the side of the island is about the size of a tennis court with what looks like a rock railing around the outside edge. Someone had put in a lot of effort to make it look natural. The nearly full moon shone over the water and even faintly illuminated the villas below. It really is breathtaking.

Lost in thought I didn't hear the doors open behind me so I jump slightly when I hear a warm voice with a Slavic accent say, "It really is beautiful up here isn't it?" I turn to see Tattianna Shultzinger coming to join me by the rim. She smiles, "Sorry didn't mean to startle you, but when I saw you headed this way, I couldn't resist the chance to get you all to myself for a moment."

Momentary panic sweeps through me. Maybe she wasn't as ok her husband's reaction as I had earlier thought. Was this a chance to warn me off in private? As if. Yeah, he's good looking enough and a bazillonaire to boot, but he's so sexist and arrogant. Why couldn't the man just show some social consciousness? The opulence of this place being just one example. "I was just lost in thought. You really do have a beautiful view here." There, maybe that was placating enough. Might as well just clear the air. "I'm sorry if I've been a disruption for you. I'll be going home soon."

"Oh, I'm certain MU will be the duller for that. The dress is beautiful on you by the way. My Ulli told me he was the one who recommended the designer to you. I told him whatever I was paying him to double it. I don't know how we ever lived before Ullies," she smiled and seemed perfectly relaxed and at ease.

I chuckled despite myself. "Oh, mine has been a real mixed blessing. He's been helpful, but he's always so shocking... "Then when I saw the dress... well I'm used to something a little more... um conservative. I assumed Mr. Shultzinger was... I don't know... He enjoys testing people." I concluded lamely. I couldn't very well say, 'I thought your lecher of a husband was grooming me for a private dinner and more'.

She did laugh openly and warmly. "Oh that he does, but he's also got an eye for attractive women, and with his not completely undeserved reputation... I'll bet you were, shall we say dubious to say the least." She looked completely at ease and even a bit conspiratorial, though she seemed to not be offended. "Speaking of my illustrious husband and Ullies, you had said you wanted an interview. I will accept over lunch tomorrow. One condition."

"Thank you, but what condition?" I was suddenly feeling a bit worried.

"I get to interview your Ulli at the same time, but anything he tells me is off the record. You can hear it but not report it to the world." Her face was completely serious.

"Um ok, but don't you have your own Ulli?"

"Sure, but mine has the personality matrix that has grown to me. You have the one who's essentially my husband's subconscious." She looked positively wolfish, as if she had a long sought-after prize near at hand.

"Oh, I see... I think... so when my Ulli was first activated, he was acting and responding exactly like Mr. Shultzinger would have expected him to act. You think by interviewing him you can learn things about him. I'm not sure I'm ok with that." I really was conflicted. On the one hand, Shultzinger was a sexist pig, despite his obvious looks and charm. On the other hand, this would be a breach of trust.

Tattianna smiled and shook her head, "I knew I liked you for a reason. Looks like Michael was right to grant you the interview. I am not trying to pump your Ulli for information to use against Michael. Just to learn more about him so I can better know him. He gets shy about some subjects and I'm curious. I love him and would never seek to harm him, but there are some things I think he's embarrassed to discuss even with me."

I still wasn't sure, though she seemed completely genuine in the request. "Ulli, is it ok with you if Ms. Shultzinger asks you some questions?" I waited for a reply, but it was slow in coming. "Ulli, can you hear me?"

"Yes, sorry, it was just taking me a moment to go through the permissions chain. You see, Mike set me to reply to questions into his personal life with, 'Ask Mrs. Shultzinger'. However, there are no privacy settings against anything Mrs. Shultzinger asks. So yes, I will gladly conduct the interview with her." Ulli finished sounding much more comfortable by the end of the sentence.

Tattianna got caught by a fit of the giggles. I never even suspected that could happen. I felt a little uneasy until she recovered enough to explain why. "He outsmarted himself. Oh, I so love it on the few times this happens." The giggles started fresh again and were contagious because I found myself grinning like an idiot right along with her.

"What do you mean out smarted himself?" I asked when she could breathe normally again.

"A man with his reputation, and a reporter wanting to dig up dirt, he just assumed if Ulli told you to talk to me about it you'd drop the line of questioning. I'll bet it's worked for him before. He never thought about me wanting to know about our life from his point of view. Oh, I am so much looking forward to lunch tomorrow" she all but clapped her hands like a schoolgirl. "Still, we need to get back in for dinner, but let's have a little fun at his expense shall we? Let's give our clever boy a little food for thought." With that, she held out her arm for me to take. I did, and she cuddled up to me close as if we were lovers on a moonlight stroll. "We walk in like this and he'll be over thinking it throughout dinner. Between that reaction he had to you in that dress earlier and the frustration he had with the interview, yes we will, how do you say, have his wheels turning over time? No?"

I couldn't help it this time. I giggled. Yes, most men would find this something to occupy their thoughts. "Won't he know you better? I mean, for as you say his not completely undeserved reputation yours is spotless."

"Oh, we've had a longstanding agreement since just before we got married. It was another time he slightly out foxed himself. He said that he believed in complete equality. He could date other women and I could date other women as well."

I couldn't just let that one slide. "Oh, men are such pigs."

She giggled, "Oh yes but such cute little piggies. Besides, while that isn't my normal inclination, I do have a very few truly special friends... He was shocked the first time he met one of them. Though, to his credit, he handled it very well. We've even interviewed a couple of nice young women to join the family, but there has always been something come up."

My reporter senses just registered a ten on the Richter scale. This kind of revelation directly from the source could make me a career. As a gossip columnist, not a tech blogger, but still. Honestly, it wasn't much of a temptation. I really did like Tattianna and really hoped we could be friends. So, mirroring her cuddly posture, we walked back into the party and toward the tables in the center of the room. Shultzinger did do a double take when he noticed us. It was all I could do not to giggle and give it away.

Dinner

We walked in and Tattianna escorted me to a table near the head table. There were already seven people arrayed along one side. As we approached, the four men all stood courteously. "This is my husband's guest this evening, Ms. Elaine Winters. She's a journalist in America. Please make her feel welcome, as I need to make my way over to Michael. I think the first course is about ready to be served."

With that, she kissed me on both cheeks in the European style and wandered off to the main table next to ours. I smiled at my dinner companions, Commodore Whetherby, an elegant woman by the name of Dr. Lillian Shaw, what I assumed to be her husband a Dr. George Shaw, a very young woman Deborah Reynolds and her apparent date Lt. Michael Webber in a uniform similar to Commodore Whetherby's except with a silver shell on the collar rather than a trident, also an older couple Yohannan and Yevette Rood. The Commodore formally pulled out a chair beside himself and in a surprising voice said, "Ms. Winters, if you'll please join us." He sounded like James Earl Jones with a Jamaican accent.

"Thank you." I said, taking the seat and wondering what to expect next. The tables were all arranged in a semicircle around an open floor at the base of the volcano. "Nice to meet everyone."

"The pleasure is ours," said a reedy voice from older Yohanan Rood with just a trace of a German accent. "It isn't often the press is invited to these gatherings. You must have really made an impression for Michael Shultzinger to ask you here considering, his usual opinion of the entire profession." A chuckle went around the table. It wasn't unkind just in recognition of an understatement by Mr. Rood.

"Well, I just hope I don't disappoint then." I said with a polite smile.

"Oh, I doubt that," said the high clear voice belonging to Deborah. "I've actually read some of your work when Michael mentioned you were going to be here." She leaned in closer to him and you could tell their relationship was fairly new. "I've been working on a new VR telepresence program for Mr. Stutsman and it would be very helpful to get input from those who may be using the software in the real world."

I smiled at her enthusiasm. "I'd like very much to have the opportunity for that. I hope to catch Mr. Stutsman before the end of the evening to set up an interview, if possible."

"Oh, that would be wonderful. One sec…" her eyes unfocused for a moment and when she came back, she was almost bouncing in her seat. "Tomorrow at about 1530 work for you?"

I was a bit stunned, "Um sure but are you certain he'll be ok with this?"

"Of course, his Ulli is already blocking out the time on his schedule. Sorry, I forget sometimes that it takes visitors some time, getting used to having an Ulli. I don't know how anyone gets anything done in a day without one." She dimples, and she looks so young, I pull up her bio. That's because she is young. Bio says she is sixteen but also holds an associate's degree in user interface design.

About this time the rolling sound of drums filled the air and from behind the screens of vegetation on either side of the dining area come the servers all dressed as if at a luau. Two men carried a four foot long replica of a Maori War Canoe laden with fruits and hollowed out fruit rinds filled with all manner of flavored dips. As the men sat the canoe on the table, I couldn't help but notice they visibly strained to move it. The thing must weigh at least two hundred pounds. I heard a gasp off to the side and a giggle. All attempts at composure went out the window as Debbie all but clapped her hands. She looked sixteen again, but Michael didn't seem to mind. He was just helping her load several large strawberries on to the little banana leaf that served as a tray. Hitting up his bio quickly just to see, oh he's twenty-two. Not so big of an age gap in a few years, but a fairly large experience gap now. I wonder what her father thinks. As I'm thinking these things, I notice each of the men lifting off choice delicacies for their dates. Commodore Whetherby smiles back at me with one of each loaded up on two banana leaves. "I didn't know what to get, but it is traditional for the men to serve the first course. So I got us each one of everything, though from experience if we eat one of everything we'll never make it through the fourth course." he says as he sits back down depositing a leaf on the plate before each of us.

A bit shocked by the custom, but not wanting to be ungrateful, I smiled. "Thank you, but I think this could be a meal in and of itself. Did you say four courses?" Everyone at the table chuckled. It seems they had a long experience with the joys of luau food.

It really was good, but I had a question for the Commodore and since he appeared to be assigned as my date it only seemed fair to grill him. "So Chief of MU security. Must be an important job."

Commodore Whetherby nodded. "Yes, staying awake can be very difficult at times." The table politely chuckled except for Lt. Webber.

"The Commodore is just being modest. Since he's been here, we've fought off two non-state attackers and one nation state. Any of which could have been the end of us." The young lieutenant was clear-eyed and earnest.

The Commodore's voice sharpened, "That is enough Lt. Webber. That information is not common knowledge on the mainland" "

"Sorry sir, but it isn't marked as classified and maybe if the general public knew what has been tried…" he trailed off, frustrated.

"That is not yours to decide, Lieutenant! As you say, it is not classified though I probably should remedy that. I was not just 'being modest'. We are still vulnerable until the Atlantis is launched. This is a very dangerous time for us Ms. Winters. I'd rather not draw any unneeded attention for the next six months. I had asked Michael to push this whole interview idea off for another six months, but he thinks we need to make our statement now. Please, can I ask your discretion about the attacks?" He looked serious, not so much worried as wary, and most of all he looked tired.

"Well, I'm not here to put folks in more jeopardy. I didn't realize there had been actual attacks." I shook my head and rethought my earlier estimate of how cushy this job might be. "Can you at least tell me what happened? If it comes up, it is always better to have facts to answer with than speculation to guess at."

The Commodore held my eye intently for a moment, then sighed. "Probably true, though facts can be twisted by those who want to pursue an agenda. Still, if Mike trusts you, this is not on the record conversation, though." And he stared at me hard and impassive until I grudgingly nodded. "Ok, about eighteen months ago, as we were passing near the coast of Mexico, about two hundred small boats appeared on the horizon. We sent out drones to intercept and noticed they were all heavily armed. From details we learned later we believe them to be members of the Zetas Cartel. We repeatedly broadcast both by radio and loudspeaker from the drones for them to break off and return to the land. They ignored all attempts to get them to turn back. Once they were within rifle range, we sunk the lead boat. This did not persuade them to break off the attack, so, using our anti missile defense lasers, we sank all the boats." He said it as if he was talking about the weather, but I could hear the exhaustion in his voice.

"So, what did you do with the prisoners?" I ask.

"There were none. Perhaps some of them made it to shore, but it is a long swim as we stay in international waters so as not to threaten or encroach on any nation's territorial waters." Again it was delivered in the same dead voice. I was stunned. My mind couldn't grasp leaving close to a thousand men to drown.

"But there were two hundred boats. That would be nearly a thousand men." I said, trying not to make it sound like an accusation.

He just nodded, "Very nearly. Certainly more than I had troops to guard them." He wiped his hand over his bald scalp in what seemed to be a long and ingrained mannerism. "There was an attack from the South American coast about three weeks later. Two old Soviet era Hind gunships. Maybe from Venezuela or more likely, from Columbia. I don't think they were government sponsored though, but the lead helo launched two air to sea missiles. They were fortunately intercepted. The helo's armor was too thick for the lasers to do much to it, but lasers are very precise instruments and rotors aren't armored. The lead helo went into the Pacific, his wing-man was flying very erratically as he went over the horizon back toward the land."

He looked at me again, as if waiting for a response. The entire table was silent. The noise of the rest of the party was a dull hum as the impact of his words hit me. With a deep breath, he started again, "Last month we had our most serious challenge. It was an Iranian sub. Lasers don't work under water, but our radiation scanners determined the small craft had nuclear materials on board. I suspect it was a small tactical nuke in a torpedo, though Janes denies they have that technology. So perhaps they were simply going to sacrifice the sub on a suicide mission. Either way, with a specialty weapon developed in part by young Webber there, we were able to disable the sub before any damage could be done." He looks at me very seriously, "These are not accidents. If we can be destroyed before the Atlantis comes online, then the powers that rule the world think they can put the genie back in the bottle. If they can't, it could be two hundred years before they can subvert and subjugate us again. The national governments know they will end up going the way of kings if people have a choice to live without them. They will not let that happen if they can avoid it. Fortunately, they can't just openly attack us except through proxies or risk losing legitimacy. Don't doubt the first two attacks were the American CIA covert ops, and the third was a FSB project."

I looked at him, stunned. "Why didn't any of this make the news?"

He shrugged. Too many of his own years spent in black ops seem to have left him with few illusions about 'news' reports. "Who would have benefited? America is officially calling us tax dodgers. The Iranians need to appear as sane and rational as they can after the whole Beirut incident. If no one benefits from the story it never gets told. We need to keep it all quiet until after the launch of the Atlantis. Once there are two of us, it will be much harder to solve the sovereign island problem by simply sinking it. My counter part on Atlantis has caught four separate sabotage incidents. So for luckily none have been successful."

This was sure not what I had thought dinner conversation would be about. I looked around and during the Commodore's tale the second course had arrived. The other women at the table had already gotten their dates served, and I stood to get ours. After dredging all this up, the least I could do is keep to custom and serve the next course. It was a delicious grilled fish and a spiced rice dish. I looked over. The older couples looked thoughtful. Debbie just looked a bit scared as she clung to the young lieutenant for comfort.

Sitting the fish down in front of the Commodore, I caught his eye, and he smiled sadly at me. "Sorry to have such a dark dinner conversation, but you wanted to know."

I sighed, "Yeah I did, and yeah I still do. Thank you for trusting me with the truth. I won't abuse that trust." I tried to hold his eyes but in the end couldn't. There was just so much responsibility there, so much weight. "Maybe we should change the subject?"

Yvette Rood piped up, "That's actually a good idea. How about we talk the Doctors Shaw into telling us about this latest breakthrough I heard about this morning?" She looked over at them expectantly.

The couple look at each other, both motioning to the other to explain, but finally George nods and begins. "Well, in layman's terms we figured out how to create an organ outside of the animal. In this case, we will grow a cow udder. No need for the whole cow now to have our milk, butter, and cheese." He smiles. "Take the fish you're enjoying now. It was grown just as the muscle. No brain, no bones, nothing to waste. Only the muscle was grown and then served. Much more efficient and productive, and if I do say so myself more humane. Now we can supply the entire city with dairy products and take up a room only about a fifth of the size of this one." He waves his arms around to emphasize the excess of space.

The Roods were looking at each other and you could tell that years of experience were making communication unnecessary. "So, milk without the cow? How long before you can scale up production for other markets?" Yohannan asked with interest.

Lillian shook her head sadly. "It's not about scaling up. It is about overcoming regulatory hurdles. This will never fly in Europe with the anti-GMO sentiment that is prevalent there, nor in the US where the FDA and USDA will want ten years of expensive testing. Not to mention what the dairy farmers' associations will do when they find out. India has a whole host of religious and cultural issues. That really only leaves China and Japan both of which have a very high percentage of the population that is lactose intolerant. The current market for the dairy application will mostly be on the new islands like here on MU and when the Atlantis launches."

George smiled, "We are working on a marketable application, though. Spider silk. True bulk production of commercial grade spider silk will revolutionize the world. Unfortunately, milk was much easier to produce. The spider silk still needs to be spun to be useful and while the proteins are easy to make in bulk with this process, spinning it properly has proved to be more of a challenge."

Yves rubbed her chin thoughtfully. "How long before it is resolved?"

George shrugged, "Could be a breakthrough any day, could be harder than we expect and take several years. Either way, I expect no longer than three years out."

Yohanan rubbed his hands together. "I think we need to see this. Don't you Yves?"

His wife shook her head. "I don't know. Three years in this environment is a long time, but yes we need to at least see what you've accomplished. That is, if you're still needing investors," she added. Smiling because she knew it was a stupid question. Everyone needed capital to get a new business off the ground. Especially if they wanted to keep it from being bought up by a competitor just to keep it off the market.

George smiled, "Tomorrow morning would work well for us, say around nine thirty?"

"Mind if I invite myself along?" I asked, expecting to be

politely refused. "The tech is interesting, but to help my readers understand the venture capitalist method in action would prove quite useful."

Everyone looked at each other for objections and Lillian spoke up, "It could be the kind of publicity we could use?" Nods all around and my morning interview spot was thus filled.

The servers came around again and removed the remains of the second course, and the entertainment began. Rushing to the area between the tables came fire eaters and fire dancers. The music was incredible and the young men and women rushed about in a whirl of flame. This was every bit as much an art form as any ballet I had ever seen, but with the added element of fire everywhere. For fifteen minutes, the entire floor was a whirl of activity and then just as suddenly the fire went out and they were all running off in different directions. I couldn't help it. I clapped. I was just glad to see I wasn't the only one.

Four large serving men carried in an iron bull's head, steam escaping through its nostrils. The smell of spiced beef wafted up through the entire room. Servers arrived at the table with a small hibachi grill and asked how we liked our steaks. Each one grilled to taste right there at the table with sauteed mushrooms. It was phenomenal. So by this point, I just had to ask. "So how does one send compliments to the chef around here?"

Debbie giggled a bit. "Which one? Each course has its own chef. They prepare the dishes in advance and record what they do for the computer and the computer here then performs the exact same actions so everyone gets the same quality meal. This course was prepared by Jordan Pharaoh, in England."

I gasped, "You mean that guy that yells at everyone on TV?"

Debbie grinned, "The very same. The first course was by a vegan chef in Seoul. The second was by a French chef in Paris. Dessert will be by an Argentine chef. Thanks to the software I'm helping to develop, none of them had to leave their very own kitchens to do it. Who knows, in a few years, you may even be able to order this same course in your favorite local restaurant." She was beaming with pride in accomplishment, but you could tell it was well earned. I caught another meaningful glance between the Roods and just grinned back at Debbie.

"This place is full of surprises. I had asked Mr. Shultzinger, 'what's next?' but after this dinner I'm left wondering what won't be next." I said in amazement. Was surprised to hear the deep voice next to me speak up again.

"That is why they worry. This genie is almost out of the bottle and the world will never be the same. Those who were doing the best under the old system rarely react well to change." I looked over and while his face was still serious his eyes were shining with pride? Hope? Hard to tell, but you could see he was a genuine believer in what MU was all about.

I caught Tattianna looking my way. She held my eye for a second and raised an eyebrow. I wanted to laugh; I wanted to cry what I did instead of manage a bewildered smile. She seemed quite satisfied with that and returned to her conversation at the other table.

Desert finally arrived and was surprisingly simple. Caramelized bananas, covered in whipped cream and drizzled with raw cane sugar. Amazingly, it topped off the meal very well. Try as I might to restrain myself, I find I have still over indulged. Surprise!

Answers and other useless facts

As dinner is finished, people rose and mingled again. Commodore Whetherby offers me his arm. "Will you accompany me?"

I take it. He's been nothing but a gentleman all evening though one can't help but see the controlled violence seething just below the skin. He's making small talk but seems to guide me with a purpose. I start to ask him why, but Ulli takes this minute to dart into one hut ahead of us. Distracted for just a moment I realize that I too am being guided toward this little hut set into the wall. As my eyes adjust to the dimmer lighting, there sits Michael Shultzinger and two other men. They rise by reflex as I join them in the small hut. By their VR name tags, it is Douglas Burg, the brain-computer interface guru and Dr. Steven Saunders PhD. 'systems design engineer'. "Gentlemen," I say quietly, nodding to them. "I take it my finding my way here wasn't happenstance?"

The two look somewhat guilty, but Shultzinger just grins broadly. "Well no. If I'm out on the floor in full view of the crowd, someone will demand my time for some 'crucial' project or other." His tone changed while his hands made the air quotes. "What's worse is it probably is crucial enough that I'd start helping them with it, and you'd never get to finish your interview."

"Ah, I see. Well, thank you then." I smile politely and find a seat along the opposite wall. The little nook is comfortable and intimate and well sound proofed. Even speaking in mild conversational tones, I can hear each of them clearly. "Acoustics are quite impressive here." I mention as I try to settle myself, without my recent over indulgence becoming too uncomfortable.

"They are designed for just that purpose, Ms. Winters." says Dr. Saunders. "This way, conferences can be held in the main room while allowing all parties a modicum of privacy and security as they need."

"Also makes it easier for your mics to pick up what they are saying." and I arch an eyebrow.

Dr. Saunders and Mr. Burg both look as if they are going to get very offended, but Shultzinger just laughs loudly and honestly. "Wouldn't do much good if that were the case." He smirks at me, "Ah, a doubter I see. Try calling for your Ulli. Or making a phone call." He sits back with a smug look as I realize I'm electronically cut off from anyone outside of this hut. "Dampening field. Keeps all the would be spies honest." He shakes his head. "With corporate espionage being what it is, CEOs can be every bit as paranoid as National Governments. This way everyone can speak without concern that it will show up outside of channels later." He shrugs and waves his hand. "For tonight, it just gives us a little peace and quiet to finish up the interview, as I promised you I would."

"And these gentlemen are here to protect you from lil' ol' me?" I say with a smirk.

"Something like that. Actually, each of them wanted to meet you briefly and offer you a tour of their facilities. They won't be staying for the interview proper." He nodded to the men on either side of him. "I'm just their means for an introduction." He smiled calmly completely failing to look innocent.

Dr. Saunders took that as his cue and stood up. "Would you like a tour?"

"Uh of course... What do you do?" I tried not to sound too foolish.

"I oversaw the actual design of the Island and its systems. In many ways, this is as much my baby as Michael's. "

Shultzinger laughed again. "Don't let Hobbs hear you say that."

Dr. Saunders chuckled and cocked his head, denoting agreement. Seeing my puzzlement, he explained. "Mr. Hobbs is the chief engineer and to hear him tell it this is HIS island and the rest of us just get to come along for the ride." Chuckles all around again, "Still, he IS very good at his job, so we wouldn't want to let him know that the rest of us might think otherwise." Nodding politely, he heads toward the door, "I'll have my Ulli contact yours and make the arrangements," and with that he ducked out.

Mr. Burg then stood and turned toward me seriously. He was always serious in every news report I had ever seen him in. Not sure I ever saw him smile. The nick name everyone used behind his back was Burg the Borg. It really seemed to fit with his personality and his profession. "I take it you know my work?" I nodded, and he continued, "Good. Mike has said it may be beneficial for you to see some of it before we move to our own island. I will have my Ulli contact yours for scheduling." He nodded at me and at Shultzinger and said, "I bid you good evening." and walked out briskly.

"Suppose we should get to business then," I said as there were just the two of us left. "Will my recorder work with the dampening field?"

He just shook his head. "No, and I won't pretend that wasn't intentional as well." He rubbed his hands over his face and for the first time I could see the strain he was under. "I gave some real thought to that question you asked earlier today. I was urged not to answer it, at least not seriously. This is my compromise with Nigel." He scratched his chin absently, "You met Nigel at dinner I take it." I nodded, "Well he is a professional paranoid and I love him for it. My wife and I owe him our lives several times over, as do the citizens of MU on at least three occasions."

"He mentioned the attacks." I said quietly. Shultzinger's eyebrows shot upward in surprise. "It wasn't his choice. It was something Lt. Webber brought up. I kind of felt bad for the Lieutenant, as he was answering my question and took a real dressing down from the Commodore."

"Don't worry too much about Webber. If his mouth got him in trouble with Nigel, then he probably needed a talking to. Good kid, but green and trusting. Still, I want you to understand when I say this answer is off the record. I mean it is OFF the record. However, I think you need to know about it. Besides, in the long run, it may help not only your story but those who read it. If you're as good at this as Ulli thinks you are, you'll be able to convey the information without getting a directly attributable quote." He leveled a stare at me that could peel paint. Uncharacteristically, it didn't incite instant rebellion in me but made me grudgingly respect his honesty with me. "OK, no argument and no trying to lawyer the rules. OFF THE RECORD."

He just nodded. "What is coming next is disruption. Not in one area, but in all areas. Over the next fifteen years, the world is going to experience more technological growth. Well, that's an understatement, more than it has since the discovery of fire." He paused to let that sink in. "I know I don't have to explain the Singularity to you, but do stories about it. Warn people what is coming. The powers that be, in the now, benefit from how things are now. They want to shape what will be and are pushing a very specific, and in my opinion very dystopian for most people, future. At least in the long run." He paused again to think of an appropriate analogy. "Think of the differences in how the industrial revolution was handled in the Soviet Union vs. America or even the differences between America and the EU. History may not repeat, but it rhymes. And this next few decades will determine the future for this paradigm and influence all others that come after it. As a species, we've heard this tune before many times as we move from one type of society to another. They will do whatever they can do to stop, failing that slow, failing that shape to their benefit the change that which is coming. We will be much safer once the Atlantis launches in six months, until then..." he just shrugs and the weight of the entire future is on his shoulders. The thing is, it isn't an act for my benefit. It is a rare glimpse behind the act. For the first time since I met the man, I feel the urge to 'make it all better' for him. For the first time, I think I see what a woman like Tattianna must see in him. That makes all the rest worth it to her.

He looks up and catches my eyes with his. While his face is tired, his eyes blaze with determination. "So tell them. Tell them often. Just for the next six months, don't tell them I said so. Until the Atlantis launch is complete, they can't know that I know what it is all going to mean until it's too late to just sink us and be done with it. If it kills me though, mankind will enter this new world FREE." He concluded with a vehemence and a conviction that was utterly compelling.

I was frankly speechless. I didn't doubt that he believed that, and to be honest, sitting there in the darkened room with him, in that moment, I believed it too. The interview was over. I had everything I needed for a blow out story, and most of it I knew I wouldn't tell. At least not directly. "You have my word. Honest report, but nothing of this part of the interview goes out until after the Atlantis is fully up and running."

He nodded and spoke not another word. I left him sitting there, lost in his own thoughts.

CINDERELLA

I left the little alcove hut. Ulli pops up into my sight. "So how did it go?" he asks.

I shake my head a bit to clear the cobwebs. "Oh, I learned a lot, but as far as for the article, not too well. I'll think of something before I have to post up my article, but there is so much of this story I want to tell that I promised I wouldn't. Do you know where Tattianna is?"

Ulli does a little dance while he's thinking or probably more accurately communicating and says, "Her Ulli says she's with David Rosen out on the terrace. Her Ulli also says she would appreciate you saving her. Mr. Rosen tends to drone on and on about economics. Interesting for ten minutes, but she's been there for twenty-five." Ulli takes off, leading the way like a hunter on the prowl.

Suppressing a smile at his antics, I follow him out onto the terrace. Sure enough, there are half a dozen people clustered in small groups by the rail looking out at the moonlight on the water. As I walk toward them, I sub vocalize to Ulli, "Explain to her Ulli that I think she probably wants to check on her husband. He was in an unusual mood when I left him. Be subtle, and I'll gladly take her place talking to Mr. Rosen. Perhaps it will make a good side piece for the main interview."

As I get close enough, I hear David Rosen saying, "... so when the Atlantis comes online and its currency begins to trade, our Sovereign will take a bit of a hit. If you and Michael buy some puts on it at that time, you should see no loss and, when our Sovereign recovers as the general public learns that they are not built the same, you can make a killing on the way back up." He nodded, and I took this as my opportunity.

"Tattianna, sorry to interrupt, but I think Mr. Shultzinger was looking for you. Oh Mr. Rosen, it's good to meet you! I was hoping to get the chance before I left." I put on my most charming smile. It usually works, but who knows David Rosen probably had women smiling at him or at least at his Sovereigns quite regularly.

Tattianna nodded gravely. "That is a wonderful idea, David. I'll have to make certain Michael understands. In the meantime, I should go find him." She smiled brilliantly at me, "but I think I'm leaving you in excellent hands while I'm gone. Elaine is quickly becoming one of my favorite people. You really should explain to her what you were just telling me. Who knows if she can make the rest of the world understand then the Sovereign may not drop as you fear." One more blinding smile directed at me and she was gone before either of us could say a word.

Mr. Rosen looked after her as if he certainly was not done explaining whatever it was they had been working on, but then bowing to the inevitable (as a side note, I feel a Tattianna leaves many people feeling like that); he turned to me and put on a polite smile. "Certainly, Ms. Winters, I will be happy to make a few moments to speak to a pretty young companion such as yourself."

My first thought was that condescending PIG! Then I realized it probably wasn't chauvinism as much as he just discounted the intelligence of everyone he met. Ok, I can use this. "Please call me Elaine." I smiled and batted my eyes at him. Trying not to overplay it but judging by his reaction, it was mostly what he expected, even if I had gone over the top with my performance.

"Certainly, and you must call me David. These informal parties are so much better for conversations if we leave behind all the formalities." Again, his smile was polite, but his eyes had a dread in them of a conversation he thought would be so completely beneath the dignity of his intellect.

Got you now sucker. "Why thank you David, I couldn't agree more." I joined him at the rail, leaning on it and letting my hair dangle down to blow in the gentle breeze. "I heard something about the Atlantean Sovereign as I came up? Surely it would be a good deal to get your hands on some early after seeing how the MU Sovereign has appreciated over the last few years?"

He sighed long and slow. "That is going to be the conventional wisdom when it begins to trade. It is however not even remotely the same situation. The Atlantian Sovereign is designed to be a currency and medium of exchange, not a store of value." He looked at me to see if I was following. While I wasn't quite ready to shed my sorority girl act just yet, I nodded and put on my most attentive look. "Well, there you go. So the Atlantian Sovereign begins trading. People stop investing as much in the MU Sovereign so that they can 'get in on the ground floor' so to speak. Soon enough, the reality of the currency will become obvious, and then everyone will want to get out of it as soon as possible and it will tank as people try to all get out at once. All of this volatility makes currency options the ideal way in which someone in the know can clean up." He shakes his head as if disappointed. I can't tell if it is a concern of missed opportunities or if it is because people will make an economic mistake.

I sort of drop my air head pose now. I've got to make sure I understand this. "So let me make sure I've got this straight. The Atlantean Sovereign isn't like the MU Sovereign, but people will buy it because they think it is. Then when they find out the truth, it will drop like a stone. You want to make money when this happens because you know what you're selling is faulty?"

He sighs heavily and shakes his head. "It's not faulty it is just designed different for a different function and philosophy. A hammer is not a wrench, but both are called tools, so those who don't know better will assume they are the same thing. People who don't know that will make bad choices. I just want to take advantage of the situation."

I can't help it. This seems so wrong. "But you know better, so you're going to cheat them. So how is that not like, I don't know, insider trading or something?"

"Young lady, I am not cheating anyone." True anger flashing in his eyes. "They don't have to buy the Atlantis Sovereign if they don't want to. The problem is most of them will think it is a get rich quick path, and will buy it with no knowledge of what they are buying." He took a deep breath and continued more calmly. "If I knew this and they couldn't know it, then yes that would be insider trading. Though the rules for currency trading are a bit different, still it would be unethical, but we'll leave that aside for the moment. They could know, should know, before they buy the Atlantean Sovereign, and would know if they would simply study the matter. Many won't, though. They will be foolish enough to buy something that they don't understand, and will lose money on it. All I am doing is picking up the money they foolishly threw away." He still looked a bit offended, but you could tell he also was more engaged now that I was asking him questions.

"Ok, I suppose that makes sense. So I guess the next question is what makes them different? Mr. Shultzinger said that MU Sovereigns were real money because they represented the stock held by the government of MU for the businesses that are here. I sort a get that, though I don't claim to understand it fully. How is the Atlantis money different?"

His eyes glittered. "See if the fools would ask themselves that very question, and find out the answer. They too could pick up the money lost by those who don't do their homework! Since you're asking and you seem genuinely interested," he paused to look at me. To my surprise, I was actually interested. How could money work differently? After all, wasn't money money? Seeing he still held my attention he continued. "Atlanteans are not going to have money. That is, they will not have a store of value. Their Atlantean Sovereign will simply be a currency, a medium of exchange. Think of it as a way to keep track of who owes who what. Similar in many ways to the US Dollar, though the US would never admit that." He seemed genuinely amused. Did everyone think badly about the dollar? Mr. Shultzinger didn't think it was real money, and David obviously wasn't impressed. "What the Atlanteans will do is distribute their currency evenly among their citizens at the beginning of every year."

"Oh, so a Universal Basic Income like Mike Zuckerman is pushing with his new Make America Greater party?" This seemed like a good idea. If Zuckerman ran for president again, he'd have my vote.

"Um not quite. Sort of, but there is a big distinction that will make the Atlantian plan more likely to succeed. Even if I'm a bit biased, as it is the part I insisted upon in the formation meetings. See if Zuckerman ever gets his way, the value of the US Dollar will just go down and down and down, or in the way you'll see it prices will just rise faster and faster. Too many dollars will be created and just like rare diamonds are valuable, but common sand isn't as the dollars become less rare they will also be less valuable." He stopped again to make sure I understood. Well, I did, at least sort of. I wasn't sure he was, but I didn't know of any way I could prove he was wrong, so I thought about it for a moment and nodded. He continued, "The Atlantian Sovereign will be intentionally lowered in value by 10% from its face value every year. This will be done each day by an incredibly small, almost unnoticeable amount. It isn't unfair because it is well published that this is the case, but people, again they don't do their homework." He looked at me again, waiting for an interruption. I wasn't sure it was fair, but I wanted to hear more at this point, so I nodded. "So if they issue 100 Atlantian Sovereigns at the beginning of the year, by the end of the year there will only be 90 Atlantian sovereign in actual circulation. Most Atlanteans won't miss the 10% because they will get the new funds disbursement and have 190 Atlantian Sovereigns. By the end-of-year two, the first 100 will now be 80 and the second will be 90 and the new disbursement will be 100. So that by the end of ten years the full amount of the first disbursement will be gone. There won't be too much money chasing too few goods and services, so they won't see the price spikes after say year eleven or twelve as things normalize and everyone gets used to the new system." He nods his head as if he's said something very profound here. I confess I don't understand it all, but it seems weird but workable. He looks up and catches my eye. "Where things are going to go badly for those who buy the Atlantian Sovereigns and expect them to act like MU Sovereigns. Instead of appreciating in value, eventually they become worth nothing. There is absolutely no point in saving them. They are meant to be spent. It is a way to kick up the Velocity of Money." He stops and takes a breath at this point. "Look that up. If you don't understand it, your Ulli can help." Then he continued. "So Atlantian currency is meant to be spent and spent repeatedly. They plan this because they will fund their necessary government functions with a small sales tax. The more often the money changes hands, the more money comes into the

Atlantian Treasury. The more often the money changes hands, the more economic activity is going on. They hope that this will allow them to have vast economic growth. The fact that it can't be just passed on from generation to generation by its disappearing nature will give each generation a reward and reason to produce, yet will make sure that even the least citizen of Atlantis will have his stipend to have his necessities taken care of. I don't know that it will work, but it gives it the best chance to." He grinned a bit mischievously, "I don't intend to move to Atlantis any time soon, though I do wish them the best of luck."

"Um, I don't claim to understand all of that, but it seems like a fair system." My head really was spinning, but the more I examined it the more I thought it was very humane. "What I don't get is why will it make the MU Sovereign drop in value, even if only for a little while?"

"Ahh, that one is easy. The people of the world have a finite amount of money to invest in foreign currencies. So if they think that the Atlantian Sovereign will have a rapid rise in value, the way the MU Sovereign did, they will buy the cheaper Atlantian Sovereign more and the MU Sovereign less for a time. Value of the MU Sovereign on the open market will drop, not its intrinsic value but its perceived value." Again, he stopped to be sure I was following. It amused me how passionate he was about this. Still, there is a reason he has only a little less filthy stinking rich, than Shultzinger himself. I nodded for him to continue. "While this perceived value is less will be a good time to buy MU Sovereigns, because once they realize they are losing money on Atlantian Sovereigns they will sell those off, and buy back the MU Sovereigns, driving back up the price and perceived value."

"Ok, so you're not cheating anyone. Anyone who took the time to research their investment properly could know the same things you're explaining to me. Most just won't. Is that it?" I looked at him for confirmation. He seemed awfully picky about setting the system up to work, and you don't do that if you're just planning to cheat people. He really didn't seem the type, ok, so I only met him tonight, but still.

"Exactly, most won't. At the end of the day, I am simply making smart moves while they make poorly informed moves." He looked satisfied, as if he had proved he wasn't a cheat.

"But if I put this information in an article, then won't people know and not make the bad choices?"

Here he had a full, deep belly laugh. "Oh, please do! Please warn them. I'll even offer to proofread the content to be sure you've got it right when you tell them." He took a deep breath to regain his composure. "You know what will happen? Nothing different. You can give them all the tools in the world, but most people won't use them."

That seemed awfully arrogant. "They might! At least my readers might."

Again, he shook his head sadly. "Oh, some few might. The vast majority... nope. For decades, people have been trying to explain the fiat money system of the US Dollar, or the practice of Fractional Reserve Lending. No one ever pays enough attention, and then when economic crisis happens they look for someone to blame. The blame is on those who didn't bother to do their homework, but rarely is that the target of the anger. For more than a hundred years, people have been talking about the Federal Reserve Accounting Unit Dollar, or, if you prefer the acronym F.R.A.U.D. but people still trade away their most precious commodity, their finite time for them. No, I don't expect any, but a very few of your readers will head the warning, but I will still be happy to help you give the warning." He smiled sadly, then looked off to my right a bit. "Ulli, if Ms. Elaine Winters sends me an email with a story to review before publication, you are to make sure that I see it." He smiled and looked back at me with no guile only a weary sense of exasperation, "Can I do more?"

I couldn't help it. At that moment, this wasn't David Rosen, the bazillionaire exploiter. This was a man who really wished people took more interest in their own well-being but had despaired of seeing it. "No David, you can do nothing more than that." I reached out for his hand along the rail and gave it a companionable squeeze. "You are not what I expected at all. I'm very glad we've had this chance to talk. Though I have a feeling that Ulli will be explaining things to me well into the early hours."

He laughed again, "Oh it's already the early hours my dear. Look around. Everyone else has gone home."

I looked around and sure enough we were completely alone. I pulled up the clock in my AR glasses and was shocked to see it past 1AM. "Oh, I fear I may have overstayed my welcome. I am so sorry to have kept you so late."

"Not at all. I haven't enjoyed a conversation this much in months. I do think we should call it an evening, though." With that, he turned and walked away. At the last moment, he turned back to me. "I was serious about that effort to help you warn people. For what ever good it will do, send me the story and I'll help you make sure its facts are straight." And that quick he was gone.

I lingered for a moment, watching the dark water play out past the island's edge. This was not what I was expecting on this trip. "Ulli, get me home by the fastest rout. I've got to be up and to my first interview in just eight hours."

CINDERELLA WAKES UP THE MORNING AFTER THE BALL

"I used to think maybe you loved me now baby I'm sure..."

Mmmm.... Who's playing music? Don't they know I'm sleeping here? Man, I just get my eyes closed and... One eye manages to pry itself open and there on the wall screen is Ulli dancing with a beach behind him... "good morning sunshine," he says. "You've got forty minutes before you need to walk out the door for your first appointment. The shower is on and ready for you and breakfast will be on by the time you get out." Ulli says has he's strutting along the virtual beach in time with the overly cheerful music.

"oh...uhhgg..." as I roll out of the bed. There's no way I could have gotten seven hours of sleep. It was like I just closed my eyes. Rubbing the sleep out of my eyes, I stumble to the bathroom and between the amazing shower and Ulli playing DJ, I become functioning again.

I come out of the shower by the time the new song is on "Six o'clock already I was just in the middle of a dream..." I don't know where Ulli is digging up this music but it just kinda fits my mood. Oh, and what is that smell? It smells fantastic! I walk back into the bedroom, singing along with the refrain.

A freshly printed suit is waiting for me in the printer. I get just dressed enough to feel comfortable and then track down the amazing smells coming from the kitchen. "Fresh pancakes with strawberries and real whipped cream. Hot black coffee, and cold white milk with just a hint of honey in it," says Ulli, with obvious pride of accomplishment in his voice. I thought I wouldn't be this hungry after last night, but it smells and tastes amazing.

Trying to stop before I completely overdo it, "It's good Ulli, by the way where are you getting this play list?" I ask as "Twenty-five years and my life is still trying to get up that great big hill..." comes floating through the air and I find myself swaying to the rhythm.

Ulli stops his own dancing and turns the music down just enough to be easily heard over it. "Well, in part it is random, but it is randomly selected based on thirty-five separate criteria. Brain wave readings, hormone levels, context of recent or future events, time of day, blood sugar levels..."

I can't help it. I interrupt him right there. "Wait! You're reading my brain waves and hormone levels just to select a play list!?!"

Ulli actually sounded indignant. "Not just for the playlist. We use it for determining general health, menu choices, activity/exercise needs..."

"Exercise needs? No, never mind, more important is how are you getting all this information?" I ask, feeling just a bit violated.

"Well, your bio-monitor in your bracelet is one method, and the sample you give every time you go to the restroom, and of course passive scans of your temperature and respiration and ..." Ulli continues as if this is the most normal thing in the world.

"Stop! Ulli just stop. No one should know this much about me! Who else can get access to this information?" At this point, I'm feeling a bit sick.

"I can't stop. It's part of an Ulli's job to monitor and help his human. Though we would give no information out that you don't want us to. Your privacy settings don't allow me to share this with anyone but you without your prior approval, unless you cannot speak because of a medical emergency, then I can share it with the medical personnel who will treat you. Do you wish me to alter these settings at this time?" Ulli said it all with a serious tone of voice. I noticed the music had completely stopped. He seemed to be waiting for my response.

"No Ulli, it makes sense, but it concerns me that this much information is gathered about me." I still felt uneasy about it all, but it seemed to have some serious upsides, and the downsides seemed to have safe guards on them.

"In that case, you'll want to continue to get ready, as our meeting with the Roods and the Shaws is fast approaching." The music came back up with a bubbly girl band, but the magic of the morning was gone. I finished getting ready and then checked my look quick and headed out the door with Ulli leading the way.

Commuting around the island was amazingly smooth. With a population density of a major metropolitan city, you would think the traffic problems would be similar, but here it's a smooth easy walk, four elevator rides and within just a few minutes I was arriving outside of a small suite of offices. I was surprised to find the Roods and Shaws all arriving at almost exactly the same time. I sub-vocalized, "Ulli is it a coincidence we all get here at exactly the same time?"

Ulli laughed and did his little back flip, "Of course not! Ulli is very good at managing time. We talk to each other and know traffic flow patterns and where other members of a meeting are, so no one is too late or too early. Everyone is just where they need to be when they need to be there. Ulli manages time and traffic very well indeed." He said smugly. There wasn't any time to dig deeper into it though as the four others were waving to me in greeting as the Dr. Shaw was opening the door to let us all in.

VENTURE CAPITAL MU STYLE

We get in and get settled in a small conference room. Yohannan is looking restive as George and Lillian roll in a box each. These boxes are on a wheeled cart and about 3'x3'x2' with a half inch diameter hose coming off of one side. George looks at everyone and smiles and motions to Lillian who nods and puts a small syringe into a port on the back of the box. "While my lovely assistant ads the proper hormone to release the milk, I'll make sure that this end is over the proper catch basin..." at that moment the milk just started flowing down the tube and right into the catch jar. It was thick and creamy and flowing far faster than what I thought was normal from that story I did on dairy farms in high school. "What we have here folks is clean, wholesome natural milk. No additives or preservatives." He smiled really widely. "you can pasteurize it or not at this point. Unlike traditional methods where cross contamination of the milk is likely this method is clean and once set up in an industrial setting even sterile."

Yohannan's face scrunched up a bit. "So we can drink this just like it is?"

Lillian smiled, "Of course, or you can separate out the cream and make butter or cheese or whipped cream..." she shrugged to show that the possibilities were as limitless as the imagination. "These are taken right off the rack that supplies the island's dairy needs now. Once serviced, they can go right back into the production system and right back to giving about a gallon of milk per milking, and being milked four times a day."

Yves was leaning forward, looking at the milk in the glass. "You said servicing? What kind of servicing?"

George looked nervous, and Lillian hesitated only for a moment before proceeding to undo clasps of the box. "OK, only fair to warn everyone you're looking at an organ without skin so it's not the most appealing sight. Then again, neither is a cow when you know them more than from driving past them on a road trip." With that, she pulled off the cover, and it was disguising. Raw red organ suspended in a bloody nutrient solution. She spun the table to the side and pulled off a little plastic bag that was filling with a dark tar like substance. "This is the waste pack. This pack will be full after one week. Typically, they are serviced twice a week for security's sake and on average produce one hundredth of the waste a cow will produce. More than that if you count methane and CO2, etc." She replaced the waste collector and also a nutrient pack and reattached the cover.

Yves looked queasy at what was under the hood, but nodded slowly. The second box was then wheeled to the forefront, and the cover removed and a large bloody muscle was mostly filling the container. George smiles, "Yes I know it doesn't look appetizing in this form but neither does a slaughter house. This is about eighty pounds of prime steak. The muscle grown here is the tenderloin where the filet mignon is cut from. This is approximately a quarter of the meat that is on one beef cow, but about three times the prime steak cuts. Not really any hamburger here. The good news is for the price of prime cuts this is about equal to the cost of raising it on the hoof. The downside is it isn't cost effective over all unless you are on an island or in a city where land is at a premium." George looks at them both and shrugs, "Location, location, location, as the real estate people say."

Both Yohannan and Yves are looking at each other calculating. Yohannan breaks the eye contact and asks Lillian, "Dr. Shaw, you mentioned spider silk material?"

Lillian smiled and reached into her pocket. She pulled out a small disk and slid it into the viewer on the table. The wall screen lit up and there was about a twenty-minute presentation extolling the virtues of spider silk and potential uses for it. At the end, she turned to look at her guests. "This is the holy grail for our company. We can make the proteins and synthesize them in quantity. We can even turn them into a product that is approximately the same strength and ability as Kevlar. The problem is, it is only as good as Kevlar now. Once we figure out how to spin it as the spider does, then it will be many times the strength of Kevlar and will be as highly sought after as carbon nano tubes, and graphine or aero gels, like this entire island is made of."

Yohannan nods, "And to do this you need funds for research no?"

George smiles easily. "You've essentially grasped the essence. Oh, we'll eventually figure it out, with outside funds or without them, but there is a time factor here. We're not the only company to tackle this problem. We're just the furthest along. Living on MU has provided access to the type of personnel you can reliably contract for confidential work." Again, he shrugged.

Yves speaks up at this point. "If we choose to invest, we'll want the customary fifty-one percent of stock. I know it seems a lot, but it is the only way to protect our interests and the bulk of your funding will come from us I presume?"

George and Lillian look at each other and then Lillian speaks, "I understand that is the typical arrangement in Europe and America. Here on MU, that isn't even legal." She waited for it to sink in.

Yohannan barked a slight noise of surprise. "What do you mean? We were told when we applied for our visa that we could engage in investing business with citizens of MU."

George smiled politely. "Of course you can. We wouldn't have wasted your time otherwise. Remember, things are just done differently here on MU. As you may know, the government of MU holds twenty percent of the value of any company as nonvoting preferred stock. The legal maximum that a purely financial partner can hold, in the initial offering, is twenty percent of non-voting preferred shares and twenty percent of the total voting shares. Total value not to exceed forty percent of the value of the entire company. It can grow beyond that if we need to come back to you for more than your initial investment. We, however, won't need to do that as we also have a crowd-source funding method which has locked up about fifteen percent of the total value of the company."

Yves was looking pretty shocked. "How can this be! How can you expect anyone to fund you like this? It just isn't done!"

Lillian finally found her voice in all of this, "It is done, and done every day here on MU. This isn't America or Europe where being friends with a banker lets you buy up controlling interest in everyone's idea. The MU government doesn't wish to risk its twenty percent stake by allowing the providers of capital to over rule the engineers and scientists who make it work. There needs to be a balance and if you want to do business on MU, you must respect that things are done differently here. This doesn't mean we wouldn't welcome your investment, for say thirty percent evenly spread between voting and non-voting shares." She waited for their reply.

Yohannan's face was purple. It was obvious no one had put his options to him quite that bluntly before in one of these meetings. "This is outrageous! You people just don't know how business is conducted." and with that and not even looking back for Yves he storms out of the office.

◆ ◆ ◆

After the door closed behind Yves, as she chased off after her enraged husband, George shook his head. "Well, that could have gone better."

Lillian was still a bit angry herself at this point. "Oh, what do you expect when they don't do their homework?" She wiped her sleeve across her forehead. "Want to do business in a foreign nation and not learn its laws first?" I couldn't help but hear David Rosen's words echo in my mind from last night.

George snorted. "That type doesn't even realize we're a foreign country. In their minds, the way it's always been done in the Western world is how it has to be done. Yeah, we could really have used the money. It would help us with the time push, but we'll figure out how to crowd source it and we'll be just fine."

Lillian starting to calm down after George lowered the stress level in the room,"Yeah can you imagine if we'd said yes and then been in business with them five years down the road?"

George calmly smiled, "Well those kind of people are one reason business got so far off track in the first place. People who understand the money side making demands, and it makes companies more money, but it often makes lousy products."

I figured it was time to break my fly on the wall status. "George, can you explain that to me because I don't see how making more money for your company is bad for the product?"

Lillian giggled a bit, "OK I can see on the surface how that would sound illogical. It really is true, though."

George smiled at his wife. "Let's give you an example. Company A makes a widget and competitor Company B makes a similar widget. Company A uses substandard parts because they are cheaper. They also accept lower margins on their build because they know that they will make more money on selling parts to fix the cheaper ones that they used. Company B makes a quality product that is more expensive but is reliable and has a lower overall cost of ownership. Which company is run by engineers and scientists and which is run by financiers?"

I smile because I see where he's going. "Ok I get the point, if company A can grab a big enough market share, then Company B no matter how much better it is will lose out."

Lillian grinned, "VHS vs Beta-max" as she nods and then giggles again, seeing the confusion on my face.

"VHS what verses what?" I ask genuinely confused.

"George, you're supposed to stop me from using antiquated examples that show my age," she looked mock fiercely at George who just grinned. "VHS and Beta-max were two competing formats for early tape drive video. If it makes it easier for you, think of .WAV and .MP3 duking it out. In this case .WAV won even though .MP3 was clearly the better format. It was all because of machines that could only read one format. To answer your question, though, it is a real risk, but cheating to win doesn't really help you get far in life. MU's philosophy on that one is; even if we can't sell it off of MU, the citizens of MU would prefer the better format and look for a way to make it cross compatible if need be later." She shrugged. "If you want to help, when you report on this fiasco, just slip in a link to our Patreon page and maybe we'll have enough crowd source money. We won't need the big money investors."

George laughed, "I don't need money people. I've got Lillian, and she never misses a chance for a shameless plug."

She just threw a pen at him and he just laughed, and after a second or two so did she.

I couldn't help thinking to myself how different things were here. They've really tried to rethink many aspects of society and culture and finance that I'd just taken as given my whole life. I couldn't help but wonder how much of this was Shultzinger and how much was men like Rosen.

"I have a few minutes before my next meeting. Do you have a couple of minutes to talk with me?" I asked, hoping they had expected this to go longer as well.

George looked at Lillian. She smirked and shrugged slightly. "Sure, but what do you want to know that the information packet we sent your Ulli doesn't cover?" she asked.

"Well, I was going to ask something more of a personal nature if that is ok?" I met her eyes.

"We are private people Ms. Winters. I don't know that putting our personal life out in front of everyone is really what we want to do," George said.

"I understand, so how about if I promise to not use your names without your permission?" I asked, looking over at him so he could see my face and hopefully read my honest intentions there. His expression didn't leave me with a lot of hope.

"Tell you what, you do that and we reserve the right to not answer if we don't want to." he said with a smile.

"All I could ask. What I'm really curious about is why MU? What made you decide to uproot yourselves and go through the not insignificant expense to move to MU?"

They both chuckled and Lillian said, "I blame George. I didn't want to leave my home and my library and my lab, and still sometimes miss sitting in the library and smelling the books and the polished oak shelves, but even after being here only a little over a year, I wouldn't trade it now for anything."

George was smiling a bit shy and just a bit guilty. "So George" I asked. "What was it?"

George took a deep breath and let out a long sigh. "Well, for me, it was as much political as it was economic and professional." He closed his eyes for a moment and gathered his thoughts. "Here there isn't what I call the Left/Right paradigm." I'd heard this term before usually from real kooks and crazy libertarians, but George didn't strike me as a kook. "In America you have people for something and others against it, but no one for solving the problem. Let's take the whole gay marriage debate of a few years ago as an example. There were big money donations from the LBGTQ community if you were for legalizing it, and big money donations from the Evangelicals if you were for keeping it banned. So both sides went to war. The bubble slid back and forth for several years and still to this day it is a touchy subject, with both sides feeling victimized by the outcome. Here on MU, we solved the entire issue before it ever got out of hand. Religious ceremonies "marriages" are held by religious organizations. Familial Contracts are what you have between the members of your family, however you define it, and the government. This contract by law must spell out rights and obligations of all parties, both while in effect, and also in case of a breach of that contract or in the case of the dissolution of the contract. Pretty much put a big hole in the divorce lawyer business here on MU." he chuckled at that. "Still, the point isn't how it was solved rather that we didn't let ourselves get limited to only two solutions, each of which would violate one side or the other. We didn't pick left or right, but a third option that seems to work for us." He smiled at me, though he still looked like he half expected me to call him a bigot and storm out. I was uncomfortable to realize that in other circumstances I might have been tempted. "Any way, that is only one example of it. The problem is when politicians can make headlines and gather campaign donations to be for one course of action, or against it, but neither of them get votes or donations if the problem is actually solved, there is very little incentive to solve a problem."

I couldn't help but think about that. He was right, but at the same time it can't be that simple. "But if someone had a solution, wouldn't he just come forward with it? If it really was better, wouldn't it win out in the end?"

He smiled sadly. "Oh, people did come forward with this solution. The media, and the six corporations that own over ninety percent of the content that is aired, didn't want the problem solved, either. You've heard if it bleeds it leads? Well, a solution that doesn't leave either side a victim kind of becomes a non story." He really sounded sad as he said it. "Unfortunately, it is still happening just that way in America."

"So here on MU they just solved that with a government owned broadcasting company, kind of like the BBC?" I asked. I had heard that all broadcasts were government owned.

Lillian giggled, "Oh, don't let MacAllan hear you talk about MU Media and the BBC in the same breath. Yes, radio broadcast is government owned, but it is really used for emergency broadcasts only. All Media distribution here is done via the internet. Yes, the government is your ISP, but it would be better to think of it like roads and bridges back in America. Government maintenance but anyone can use it, at any time. Even more so for our internet than your roads, as driving is a privilege and requires a license, here internet access is a right of anyone with an internet capable device."

"Really? I guess I didn't realize that. So no cell phones as it's all VOIP software. No cable bill. No internet bill because it's a government funded utility? Am I getting this right?" I was a bit incredulous as in this capitalist mecca I didn't expect MU to be paying for anything but national defense.

George grinned at the look I wore. "Essentially, yes. If you want to watch a show, it's probably a couple ten thousandths of a Sovereign an episode and usually commercial free."

I laughed, "Shoot I might have moved for that alone."

They both smiled at me, though George got more serious. "It also means that news is not filtered through those six propaganda companies. Oops, did I say that out loud?" he grinned wickedly at me.

"I heard nothing for the record," and I winked at him.

"So while you may still get bias in the news sources you choose, everyone is getting news from multiple different sources, so it tends to balance out in the end. It also tends to limit some of the left/right paradigm trap we talked about earlier. MU isn't perfect, but she is doing very well for a nation not yet recognized by the other nations of the world, and barely four years old. I can't help but see the ironic humor that none of them want to recognize us, and nearly all the big players have tariffs against our goods, but yet they all want the technology we develop here. At some point, you would think they would ask themselves what is MU doing that we are not that allows such an unprecedented rate of innovation and development there? I suppose, maybe that is too much to ask from the hive mind of a bureaucracy."

I started to ask more questions, but Ulli started pointing to the clock in the lower left of my vision. "I wish I had more time to talk. This has been truly enjoyable. I promise discretion with the use of names. Thank you both for this, but Ulli is reminding me I will be late if I don't head out soon." I smiled and stood up.

They walked me to the door and wished me a good day. I couldn't help but wonder if they would find the funding they needed. I hope so. They are good people and it would be nice to see the good guys win one.

BERG'S IDEA OF ONENESS

Ulli led me through the corridors of MU along a winding path until we reached a door plainly lettered "Berg & Associates". Honestly, it looked more like the shingle for a recent law school graduate than a well-funded research program. The door opened automatically and a young woman was sitting behind the desk in what looked like the set from an 1980s movie of what a Japanese Company's lobby should look like. She smiled as she stood. "Ms. Winters, we are glad to have you here. Mr. Berg is waiting for you in conference room one, just there on your right. Would you like to have some tea served to you during the interview?"

I smiled back, feeling just a little off balance, still not quite used to everyone knowing who I was before I introduce myself. Remembering to check her virtual name tag before I reply, "No thank you, Ms. Ramos. I'm fine. Just looking forward to seeing what all the excitement is about." Then turned and headed toward conference room one as instructed. Just as expected, the door automatically opened and, true to form, the Americanized idea of an Asian board room opened before me. Mr Berg was seated at one end of the table.

He rose politely, giving me a slight half bow. It was somewhat amusing to see the adopted Asian mannerisms coming from a man who looked more like a Swiss banker than an Asian businessman. "Please come in and have a seat. I thought we would take a minute to view a small presentation first. Don't worry it is not, as they say, death by PowerPoint. It just covers some basic groundwork before we take the tour." Never a smile, just a serious look. Intensely polite, but no trace of any emotion at all.

I take my seat. It is cool black leather and chrome, and surprisingly comfortable. "Thank you for this opportunity. It is helpful to see the businesses that make MU the shining star of innovation it has become. Mr. Shultzinger was too kind to arrange this."

Berg becomes even more bland faced at the mention of Shultzinger's name. Maybe I should let that connection drop. Before I can read anything more into it Berg says, "Oh Michael Shultzinger has taken a great interest in our work, but he says it gives him the 'willies' I think was the exact term. For all of his innovative spirit, he gets very conservative when contemplating the mind." He comes as close to smirking as I've ever seen him and then makes a hand gesture and the lights dim somewhat and one wall becomes a vid screen. "Shall we get started?"

Without waiting for my reply, the screen starts some old lab footage from the early 2000s. A much younger looking Douglas Berg is assisting an older man running an experiment with white lab mice with large clunky circuit boards attached to their heads. "In this, one of the first experiments of its kind, we had two mice each with a half a dozen electrodes implanted in their brain. Each communicating with a personal computer. We would teach one mouse a trick and found the other mouse would learn the same trick in half the time. This worked no matter which mouse we taught first. Needless to say, those results with such crude tools made for some very intriguing results." The video shifts to another scene in which again there were two mice with much smaller electronic on their heads. "This experiment was from the early teens. We had increased the number of electrodes by a thousand and make their location in the brain far more precise. This allowed us to better study the brainwave patterns and improve signal interception and replication. Though by today's standards still using very crude tools, as you'll soon see." The video changed again and this time it was accompanied by EEG scans of the brains. There were four mice, and each had a part of a complex problem and only when all four got it right would they each get a treat. "This is from 2019. As you can see, it took us several weeks to teach them to get their part of the task right. The better scans of their brains allowed for even better placement of the electrodes and as a result, once we had trained each mouse on one task, we could dump any of the mice into any part of the task and they would quickly perform it." The screen shifted again, and this time it was primates each doing a more complex task. "Same results two years later with these rhesuses monkeys. Even more electrodes and only that little antenna as external evidence. By this time the US military was heavily courting us, though I had expressed time and time again I had no interest in working for them." The vid ended, and the lights came back up. "Questions?"

I couldn't help it. I laughed, "Sure, about a thousand, but I'd settle for just one before go see what you're up to now." He nodded for me to continue. "Are these later experiments talking through a computer or directly mind to mind?"

"Ah, good question. There will always be some computer interface to relay from one subject to the next. As you will soon see though, that computer can now be made quite small and in our next generation will be carried sub-dermal."

I thought about that for a second, realizing exactly how far they had come since the last interview I had seen back in the mid teens when I was in high school. He stands up and motions toward one wall, and a door I had not noticed there before automatically retracts into the wall, displaying lab facilities behind. "Shall we make a quick inspection tour?"

I nod. "Please, this has all progressed farther than I had supposed." If truth be told, worse than I feared, it gives me the 'willies' too, but best not to let on at this point. I was led into a lab filled with men and women in white uniforms that looked like they were from the old style clean rooms that used to be used before everyone just 3d printed their electronics. He leads me over to a table on which a maze is constructed. Five small white mice were in the opening compartment of the maze. He gestures to the young lab attendant who doesn't look like she can be much older than fifteen and the mice are given a signal to start.

"They each know what needs done to satisfy the maze. Watch." he says confidently and is staring at the test intently. The mice are negotiating obstacles until they come across one that the only solution requires one of them to be left behind. They quickly negotiate the obstacle and the one who was left behind just lays down off to one side, as if he knows his part in this is done for now. The rest continue on. "As you can see, they don't even attempt to bring the one that must stay behind, nor do they fight over who it will be. Before you ask, the actual method of selection is still a mystery, and it isn't the same one each time." As he was talking, the mice quickly negotiated four more obstacles, each one different from the last but each one requiring them to sacrifice one of their number to successfully negotiate the obstacle. Then finally the final mouse gets the small reward pill at the end of the maze, but all five mice are shivering with the pleasure of the reward. "Even those who didn't make it to the end share in the reward. As long as one makes it to the mild intoxicant, all of them can enjoy themselves, but only if one makes it. They seem to have figured this out."

I feel a little sick at the nature of this test, but I can understand why someone like Berg would find it fascinating. "That is pretty amazing. Is the reward something you distribute evenly?" I ask.

"No, it is simply transmitted to the mice from the mouse who actually obtains the goal. Imagine the possibilities if men could share this same level of cooperation, where success for one was success for all rather than competing with each other all the time?" he looked as if he was envisioning some glorious dream. Honestly, the thought made my skin crawl.

I spoke up, if for no other reason than to make it harder to run away screaming. "You have progressed very far indeed" "

Berg nodded again. "Oh, there is more." He nodded to the girl administrating the test and moved on to the next small lab just off to the north of this one. Not knowing what else to do, I followed.

When we made it to the new lab, there were three chimps in a large glass enclosure. There were puzzles and tests and toys strewn all about. Berg whispered quietly to me, "Careful what you say in here. We don't want to taint the testing. You'll see in a moment why I say it that way." With that, he walked over to a small desk sat on one side of the glass wall and turned on an intercom. "BoBo, who wants to talk to me? BoBo or should I talk to Lucy instead?" One chimp walked over to the little console on their side of the glass and pushed two icon buttons.

The computer generated voice says "We talk" "

Berg continued, "Yes but who am I talking with?"

Two buttons pushed again, "We Talk" "

And for the next 20 minutes, while I sat there stunned Berg carried on what can only be called a conversation with the chimps. Never once did the one speaking identify himself by name or indicate that the others weren't sharing in the conversation. Berg asked for a toy to be brought over where he could see it and one chimp he wasn't speaking to, brought it over for him and once it was placed where he could see it the chimp lost interest and went back to what it was doing before.

I felt in awe and ready to throw up all at the same time. I was glad when he motioned for us to go out a different door and right back into the conference room.

As the door silently closed behind us, Berg motioned for a chair and as I sat took a seat himself. "Do you realize what you were seeing there?"

I was afraid I was, but maybe I was overestimating it. So I just said, "I think so, but why don't you give me the details so we can be sure I'm not reading more into it than the data justifies?" Yeah, I didn't really want to talk at this point. Let's just hear the man out and maybe something he says will make it seem not so bad.

Berg nodded again, "Well each of those chimps was individually taught about a hundred and ten words each. Collectively, they each have about a five hundred word vocabulary. They were able to retain the symbols they were taught and reason out a couple of dozen more on their own. Their reasoning skills and planning skills aren't much improved, except that they act with amazing cooperation, even more so than you saw with the mice. Their intelligence differs from that of men and will never rival us for complexity, but three chimp brains are definitely better than one." He stopped and looked at me. I was trying hard to mask my discomfort.

"So they work together on problem solving. They share a vocabulary. Um... Mr. Berg, how can you be certain that they aren't intelligent enough to be considered more than lab subjects now?" I asked, wanting any excuse not to be involved in this any further.

"We've tested. Here," he said, motioning toward the vid screen, "the second half of the videos. I just wanted them to wait until you had had the lab experience to draw from." With those words, the lights dimmed and the videos of the tests started. He was probably right based on what I was seeing, but it still turned my stomach to see them so violated in the mind like this. I know lab animals aren't pets, and live very harsh lives to save our lives with the research done. Still, I wasn't sure how much more I could watch first hand.

As the vid died and the lights came up, Berg looked me directly in the eye and said as seriously as he had said anything, "I can see this troubles you. Would you care to share with me your opinion?" He just waited there, holding my eye and waiting for the response.

I blinked first. "Yes, I find it very troubling. It violates the long-held concept of identity. This is very troubling research, though as with all the things I have seen here on MU, I can see where it has its benefits as well." I added rather lamely, trying to be fair about it.

Berg just nodded. "Shultzinger was right about you." He said it as if it left a foul taste in his mouth. "Would you like to see the final testing? The one he won't let us do here on MU but will provide a separate smaller island to run the experiment on in six months?"

Honestly, I wasn't sure I could take much more of this, but how could I not? Ignorance is not bliss, ignorance is dangerous and becoming more so as our technological capabilities grow. I nodded, not really trusting myself to speak just yet. Then a thought hit me. Smaller island? Screwing up my courage, I asked him, "Smaller island? So not on Atlantis, but on another island?"

Berg nodded. "Yes, built off the pattern of the prototype for MU. It is only about the size of four football fields in foot print and with full self sustaining equipment on board has facilities for about two hundred researchers and crew. It is already built but is blocked in behind the Atlantis at the moment. Our island, and about twenty others, will be unblocked when the Atlantis launches. It's no MU or Atlantis or the soon to be Avalon, but it will be quite sufficient for our needs." Berg stood and as he gestured toward the far wall a panel slid quietly back, revealing a small passageway.

As we stepped out of the little passage, with Berg leading the way, he says over his shoulder to me, "We would appreciate you writing about us, but we really need you to keep everything confidential for ten months. Let us move to our island and try the experiment before you bring the entire world. And all of their currently unanswerable and unknowable questions on us." Not even waiting for my agreement he moved into a large room. It is decorated much like a zen temple in medieval China or Japan. Around the room were six women and four men, all completely bald, all wearing white and gray loose fitting tunics similar in cut to martial arts uniforms and over that is a long hooded back robe belted at the waist. On each head is a series of glistening sequins shining just slightly brighter than the thin coating of gel that holds them in place. Eight of them sit cross-legged on the floor while two blindfolded women practice what appears to be martial arts katas, but both are moving at a very slow pace so that it is more of a dance than a fight.

I look at Berg, but he just motions for silence, and I watch. Every so often, one participant on the outer ring sighs or loses concentration but for the most part it continues on like this for several minutes. Then, with no ceremony, it is done and the two women smile as they pull off the blindfolds. They are quickly joined by the others who've stood and walked toward them, and then once they are all grouped together they turn toward us. Berg says, "These are my equivalent of the Mercury astronauts. This is training with no implants only what can be done transdermally and it means they only sync up correctly about twenty percent of the time. Every move you saw there was actually directed by the initiates seated around the pair in the center. The seated initiates think and the two central figures move."

I am in complete shock. Even without implants, these people were able to experience an amazing level of brain to brain communication. More than communication one person's thoughts was actually moving another person's body. 'Something was just completely wrong with this', screamed every instinct I have. Instead, I swallowed hard and schooled my voice to come out as calm as possible. "That is an incredible advancement. I take it you're wanting to implant the electrodes next?"

He nodded. Each of the participants came up smiling and laughing introduced themselves to me. They all had their reasons for wanting to pioneer this new area of science, and the reasons were as diverse as the participants themselves. I had to ask, "Aren't any of you worried about the surgery?"

One woman who had been in the center of the ring smiled. "Oh, we're not going to need surgery. We now have capillary sized nano transmitters that will lodge near each neuron cluster. It is really this development that makes this all possible. For now, it is incredibly expensive to manufacture them in quantities sufficient for a human brain, but if we're successful, the cost should come down to a reasonable amount for anyone who really wants this life to be able to do so. Probably fifteen years away or so, but by then we'll already have proven its value, and it's safety."

Stunned doesn't begin to describe it. I really don't know what to say at this point. So instead of doing a reporter's job and getting more facts... I said, "Thank you all so very much for sharing this with me. I wish I had more time to spend digging in to it all further, but my next meeting is approaching and I am out of time for this trip." The looks on their faces were disappointed, but the enthusiasm that they held for the project really shown through. I felt bad, because I really could have spent an extra ten minutes with them, if only I could have stomached it without having a complete breakdown.

Berg nodded again, and motioned to the wall and the door back to the boardroom appeared. "I would like to invite you to our island in say seven or eight months so you can see our progress before you report our existence to the rest of the world. This is one of three teams of ten each who will undergo the experiment. I would like you to have a chance to interview all three teams about their experience. After they've had time to adjust to it, that is."

Trying not to break out into a run, I just nod. "I think that would be a fantastic story. Please see that my Ulli has your contact information and thank you again for this one of a kind opportunity." With that, I was back in the little reception area and out into the hall. When I was sure that the door had closed behind me, I couldn't help it. I ran.

I THOUGHT FIGURING OUT WHAT FORK TO USE WAS BAD

Fortunately for me, I only ran for about a minute when I notice Ulli jogging along beside me. He waves, "Not in that big of a hurry. Ulli will get you to your lunch appointment in plenty of time. Besides, you're going the wrong way."

I manage a harsh sort of laugh, unsure if it was at me, the situation, but most certainly at Ulli's response. I stop and look around and realize I only cleared a couple of hundred yards down the corridor. "I wasn't worried about being late, I just really needed away from... THAT" whatever that was I thought.

Ulli shook his head and did his little Ulli dance. "Oh I understand, but really you are going in the wrong direction and if you had kept going even my superior guiding abilities would have had a hard time getting you to lunch on time. So let's just hit that next tube on your left and drop down about thirty floors." With that he just started heading off that way, walking right through the light traffic that I just noticed was in the corridor at this time of the late morning.

Shaking my head to clear away the last of the fog, I follow Ulli and enter the elevator. I look around as we keep going down and people get off at different floors. A nice young couple about my age get on at the next stop, and are arguing about whose turn it is to cook dinner. That little slice of mundania here in the magical land of MU was oddly reassuring. Finally, it is my stop and I realize that we've gone deep into the island. The corridor here is narrow, and it appears mostly residential cabins, at least I assume so by the almost apartment building look to the halls. Ulli turns back in the direction I had been running from and we walk through the mostly deserted hallway and past cross corridors and past two more elevators. A rather haggard looking mother with three young children goes by telling them if they don't stop running, that there will be no desert this evening. It all seems so common, so normal after all the excitement of this trip that I almost want to just stop and watch for a bit. Unfortunately, Ulli is right, and I need to keep moving. My reservation is in about six minutes, and if I know Ulli by now, we'll be getting there just in time.

The passageway opens up in a few feet to a large open room that is crowded with people going this way and that. Little shops line the walls and I somewhat regret that there is no time to do some shopping. It looks like a shopping mall you would see in any American city, or maybe more like a well-maintained downtown business district in a small tourist town, except that it is all inside. Though it really doesn't feel closed in, the high ceilings and natural sunlight streaming through strategically placed skylights gives it an open air feel. Ulli leads me toward the little central park area and to a two story Aztec looking step pyramid. A young woman standing at the door smiles brightly and says, "Hello Ms. Winters, we've been expecting you. Mrs. Shultzinger apologizes she is running just a couple of minutes behind schedule. Would you like to wait for her in the bar, or be shown directly to your table?"

It's not even a second's hesitation. After the last hour, I could really use a drink to settle my nerves. "I'll gladly wait in the bar."

Her smile never falters, "Just this way" and she holds open the door for me and once in she points just off to the left and to, what else would I have expected on MU, a Tiki bar?

An attractive dark-haired young man with well muscled broad shoulders wearing only a grass skirt and flowers in his curly hair, smiles at me and asks, "Business drink to be ready for the rest of the day, or start the evening off early with a kamikaze?" His smile was dazzling.

I chuckled, "As good as a kamikaze sounds right about now, let's just stick with a little white wine if you've got it."

He nodded amicably. "We can or you can try the MU specialty. Blueberry wine with a pineapple twist?" He raised an eyebrow questioningly.

"Ah, when in Rome? Oh, why not? Trying new things is part of the adventure." I couldn't help it. I put the emphasis a little too strongly on adventure.

"One glass of adventure coming right up!" He chuckled as he put a bit much emphasis on adventure right back. Oh, this one is just too cute for his own good, but I bet it helps with the tips.

A bottle comes out from behind the bar, and a long pour of a deep purple liquid goes into the blender. A second later, there are a couple shots of a golden liquid and a large double handful of crushed ice. As the noise of the blender dies, he gives me a mischievous smile and pulls out an actual seashell. The 'glass' is a real seashell, a beautiful spiral held in a silvery hand. The shell is huge. It's at least as long as my forearm and as big around as the bartender's fist. The contents of the blender empty smoothly into the shell and a long pink straw is put in. He gives me a smoldering smile. "This is a middle ground. Not as debilitating as a kamikaze, but enough to make for a relaxing lunch".

I can't help it. He makes me giggle. Then I realize something, I've got no money for a tip, "Um that's great but I'm new here and so far everything has been billed to my hotel room. How do I give you a tip?"

He spreads his arms wide palms up, "Oh I can't leave you in such a dilemma!!" and again that dangerous smile. "For most people, you can simply ask your Ulli to tip them. For me, you can just buy me a drink after I get off work, say about 1730?"

That was smooth. Oh, what the hell talking to the average working stiff here will make a good angle too. "You've got it, it's a da… deal"

He smiled and looked down shyly. "Yes, ma'am it is," and then he just went off to clean up the blender. I took a sip. It was very good and was just about to compliment him on it when I heard the young lady at the door ushering Tattianna in to the bar.

◆ ◆ ◆

"I'm so sorry I am late. If you only knew how difficult it is to convince engineers to just go with the flow…" she shook her head. "Oh, I see Marcus introduced you to our national addiction," smiled radiantly at Marcus who did his best 'aw shucks' look.

"Seemed a shame for anyone to visit MU and not enjoy a blue typhoon." He smiled shyly.

"Oh, was that your motivation?" Tattianna gave him a knowing look and then a smirk, as his look turned guilty. She looks over at me. "So, are we ready to eat? Or are you soaking up more of the local, eh 'ambiance'"

I started blushing. I had nothing to feel guilty about, but you sure couldn't tell by the look on my face. She just laughed that warm, full laugh that made you think everything was just as it should be. Who knows, for her it seems like it pretty much is. "Oh, I think I've had all the local 'ambiance' that I should have for the moment." Then, maybe it was the Blue Typhoon, and maybe I just felt like being a bit sassy myself, "Until tonight, Marcus"

Tattianna giggled, and we both left the bar and a nearly stammering Marcus to the jealous glares of his male patrons. "So tell me he didn't get you with that. Buy me a drink as a tip line?" Tattianna said, smirking.

Now I did feel irked. "So you've heard it before?" I was starting to steam. What did he think I was?

"Oh, don't be too hard on Marcus. He's working for tips and the tourist girls love the line. Gotta say, if I weren't married I'd sure take him up on it," and she smiled somewhat wistfully.

"Tattianna!!" I gasped. The man was a predator using a line like that on any woman he met.

"Oh, don't give me that," she giggled. "I'm neither blind nor dead, and to not notice Marcus's smile, not to mention those shoulders, I'd have to be both." She shrugged. "I love Michael, but that doesn't mean I can't look."

"Oh, it wasn't that," I growled. "He used a line on me and I just fell for it." I was furious with him for making me feel foolish.

Tattianna shook her head, "You can't blame a young man for sticking with what works. Besides, you'll buy him a drink, and maybe spend some time with him. You're here to enjoy the island as much as to tell the story. If I was single, I would enjoy the ambiance," and she giggled a little wickedly.

Tattianna just didn't understand. Men like that are predators. I know this, and yet, I still fell into his trap. That makes me a fool.

Before I could brood any further, another young man in a grass skirt showed up and started leading us down into a large glass bowl. The tables were all at the outside of the spiral as it curled around the glass bowl of a room, allowing each table to enjoy the view of the deep ocean and the swarms of sea life that came by, to gawk at the diners as much as the diners were gawking at them. At the very bottom of the bowl was a table large enough to seat ten or so that had the ocean view all the way around it. The young man in the grass skirt pulled out a chair for Tattianna. She sat daintily upon the chair that looked as if it was grown from white choral. I pulled out my own chair, and he looked a little flustered. Tattianna spoke up, "Thank you, Devon. When you get a moment, I think I want a Blue Typhoon as well, and I think we'll just have a sampler. Elaine is a guest on her first trip to MU, and I'd like her to experience as much as the chef can reasonably accommodate".

"Of course Mrs. Shultzinger. Your guests are our guests, as always" he gave a slight bow and off he went. There was no way there was time for him to have walked to a kitchen anywhere before he was back with a Blue Typhoon in its exotic seashell chalice and just a few seconds behind him was a young woman in coconuts and a grass skirt bringing a large platter of fruits and what looked like sea weed wrapped fish, all in perfect little bite-sized pieces. And then, just as suddenly as they appeared, they were gone again.

The view was amazing, but I looked down at the table setting and was bewildered. I knew classic table manners and what fork to use when, but there wasn't a fork to be found. There were three sets of chopsticks, a spoon looking device but it was very large and had slots in it. There was a small glass half filled with either very white sand or salt with a dozen skewers sticking out of it. A set of silver tongs and even a cork screw looking device with a long handle.

Tattianna must have been expecting this reaction because she just smiled and calmly said, "Traditional table manners aren't going to do much good here. This is all so different from what you are used to, and they haven't written books on this yet for mainlanders to learn. So let's pull our Ullies out and make them visible to each other, and just not worry so much about etiquette. I really do want this to just be a chat between friends, Elaine."

What could I say to that? "Tattianna, and you know I still cringe at being so familiar with you. I enjoy your company and would deeply value your friendship. I just don't know what we have in common. You are a glamorous fashion model who went on to marry one of the most eligible men in the world, who has set you up as a queen in all but name. I'm just a girl who runs her own tech blog that nobody even reads." I shouldn't have said it but whether it was the Blue Typhoon (Curse Marcus), or the emotional wringer of Berg the Borg, the words just fell out of my mouth and hearing them I felt even more glum as I recognized them as essentially true.

Tattianna's face became suddenly stern, and I think maybe I've finally blundered. "Don't you dare think that! Before I started modeling, I was just an orphan girl in a poor country trying to recover from the horror of feudalism being replaced by the absolute stark terror of communism. You don't even want to know what the choices are for a girl in that situation. I found my way out, through a lot of good fortune and taking big chances, then working incredibly hard to make those chances pay off." She took a deep breath, "Michael wasn't mister bazillionaire tycoon when I met him. Oh, he was a reasonably successful western businessman with a truly revolutionary idea, but those fail and are bought out by the international corporations every day. I remember what it was like, and Michael too… Especially now as we wait for the Atlantis to launch." She looked tired for a moment, the first I had seen that look on her face. "The point is, you are what you make of yourself, and I see in you much of what I saw in Michael. Raw, undiluted talent. It only remains to be seen if you share his drive and determination."

I felt a tear roll down my cheek. Great, was I now going to be a blubbering idiot in front of this woman? "Thank you. I wish I could see what you see."

Tattianna smiled broadly, changing the entire atmosphere of the room. "Ah, but this is why we should be friends, so you can be reminded of your worth when you forget, no?"

I giggled. I felt like a little kid. Tattianna really had a way of making things all better, though. "You are amazing. I'm just sad I can't really use any of this for a story. If people knew this side of you…"

Tattianna waved her hand as if clearing smoke, "It's enough that you know it. I've enjoyed talking to you, and you make Michael rant and rave and think in ways he hasn't for years. He knows he's right. He's done all the research, and proved all the things he says he believes, to the point that it isn't belief with him it is just established fact. You made him start defending some of his positions again, and it's been good for him. He went back to the old proofs, and it brought new life and conviction to his beliefs. In some ways, it gave him back some of his fire, and the strength to keep fighting instead of getting worn down in this critical period. Your visit has been very good for us. We now see what it is that we are fighting for. In some ways, living here on MU, we can ignore what the world we fled was like. It is good to have a reminder from time to time. Makes one more appreciative of the good things in life."

I couldn't help but feel good after that kind of compliment. "Thank you. You think he is right too though don't you?"

She laughed, "Of course, well on most things, but let's not tell him that shall we?" and she winked at me conspiratorially. "He is right, he has done the studying. Look at what he's built here on MU. Where else has so much been accomplished in so little time?"

I nodded. I had to give her that. "I admire him too, well usually, but don't tell him I said so!" She giggled and made the cross my heart sign. "It's just he is so arrogant and sure of himself and such a... a..."

Tattianna smirked and said, "Man?"

I laughed, "Well yeah, but it's more than that... men in the States aren't like that, well few of them anyway."

We took a brief pause while the food was whisked away and more just as magically appeared. Tattianna taught me what the corkscrew looking implement was for, as she used it to pull some meat from a crustation's leg. "This is a treat for me. Michael doesn't eat this sort of thing. It isn't like he keeps the strict kosher laws in everything, but pork and shell fish he doesn't touch. I usually don't eat it when I am with him either. This is a delightful treat for me." I smiled at her and stuffed my face with another delicious dish.

Tattianna leaned back in her chair really relaxing, and said, "As to your earlier point. Not long after we got married, Michael introduced me to a woman executive at his company. She was divorced and a single mother, and generally unhappy with her life as a whole. She too thought that the men around her behaved too arrogantly. She thought they didn't respect her because she was a woman. It was she who explained to me what the term glass ceiling meant. She also told me a joke. It was funny, but it was also telling. She said 'men are like parking spaces, the good ones are taken and the rest are handicapped.'" She smiled as I broke into giggles. "As I said, it is funny. I can also understand how some single women probably look at it this way. Any way, so I am talking to Michael later, and he asked me how it went meeting her. I tell him the joke. He too laughs, and then without missing a beat replied, 'So did you tell her to learn to double park or quit bitching about the walk?'" I wanted to not laugh, but it was funny, but I also felt sick because that was such a wrong thing to say. Tattianna was just watching my reaction without comment. She raises an eyebrow and continues, "The point he was making is that they were letting others dictate the 'rules' for their life, instead of embracing who they are and going with their nature. He told me that he wanted my opinion of her, because she is up for a promotion. He was hesitant to give it to her. As he explained it, she has a view of the world that is contrary to her nature, and is striving to live up to that worldview rather than her nature. She also expects everyone else to do the same. That mindset had not brought her happiness, but rather has tainted her approach to every aspect of her life. It has really made her quite miserable, and difficult to be around. Now her expectation of a 'glass ceiling' was threatening to put one over her head. It made her difficult to work with. Not because of the work. See, she could do the job just fine, if anyone could stand to be around her long." Tattianna shrugged, "I've never experienced the things she talks about. Men usually go out of their way to be helpful, and have always treated me fairly well ever since I was no longer a child in their power, anyway." She hesitated just a second, "laugh like I just told you the funniest joke."

I was a bit surprised by the sudden change of subject, but who am I to argue with someone who's been as nice to me as Tattianna has? I let out a big laugh. I was even a bit more shocked as she leaned across the table, putting her hand on mine and leaning down toward my ear as if to whisper into it. "That 'fish' just off to the left isn't actually a fish. It is a construct. I'm betting it is Michael moving it over to check on me. This will give him a little something to ponder."

"How do you put up with him spying on you?" I was smiling, but I was really starting to get angry.

She laughed easily and pulled back, looking me in the eye. "This is a prime example of what we were just talking about. You see what he is doing as distrustful and spying. I see him checking to be sure I'm ok, or maybe just wanting to see me during a spare few seconds of his day. Of course, it is possible it could have been Nigel as well, since he is in charge of security. Including mine. Yes, he is a professional paranoid, but it has saved my life and Michael's more than once." She popped another piece of fish in her mouth, closed her eyes to enjoy it, and then continued. "You can mistrust men's natural instinct to protect, or you can revel in it, and feel safe. As a woman, I like to feel protected. The executive at his company felt the desire to be protected made her look weak, so she resented it. Not wanting to need, and not needing are two different things. Since you need it, why not enjoy the good feeling that comes with someone caring enough to fulfill that need?"

I still wasn't sure she was right, but when you put it like that, it was hard to argue with. "We shouldn't need protecting." I protested more out of habit than conviction.

Tattianna smiled her eyes twinkling, "Oh come on now, we both know better. Shouldn't isn't what is in this world." I nodded not wanting to give this up, but she was right. "When I feel protected not spied upon, I feel love for his concern, not anger at his suspicion. Which makes for the happier husband? Which for the happier wife? Speaking of which, it's time for me and Ulli to have a heart to heart." She grinned wickedly, and then the conversation became way more frank and almost graphic. I now know a lot more about one Michael Shultzinger than anyone but his wife and his shrink should know. Oddly, that hasn't diminished the man in my eyes, rather I think Tattianna may have been right. In Shultzinger's case he probably was just protecting his wife.

Lunch wrapped up, a half an hour later than expected, but fortunately, Ulli was able to confirm that Stutsman was also running late. I felt a lot like I had been on a shrink's couch by the end of the lunch, or maybe just had the best heart to heart conversation with a best girlfriend. Either way, there will be a lot of thinking to do about this conversation in the weeks and months ahead. I really hoped that I could maintain a friendship with Tattianna. She is the most amazing treasure of MU.

I even relented and had Ulli send Marcus a generous tip.

STUTSMANN INTERVIEW

Trying to get my head back in the game for this interview is difficult. I keep getting distracted by all that I have learned so far today. This is really the most amazing whirl wind adventure I've ever been on. These people really are just doing it. These people stopped asking permission. They quit seeking approval; they are just doing it. Whatever 'it' turns out to be. There is a fresh development or process or invention around every corner. Now I'm going to talk with one Roger Stutsman, the man who has redefined what artificial intelligence can mean. This could be the bigger of the interviews I've done this week and I can't seem to get my head in the game. Ulli is stalking in front of me, just leading me through the corridors as if he is on the scent of big game in the jungle. It really would be amusing if I could just kick the feeling that he at least, has his game face on.

We arrive at a nondescript unmarked door that just opens for us as we approach. Inside is a large open room, with close to seventy-five young people wandering around all talking to the air. Their VR glasses were on and everything but their work tuned out. It really is a motley crew. More than a few Mohawks and body mods mixed in with button down oxfords and even one bow tie. I think the bow tie may have shocked me more than the Mohawks, as it was the first tie of any sort I had seen on MU.

Ulli stands up from his traditional stalking position and

motions me toward a spiral staircase at the far end of the room. It winds its way up to a sort of glass enclosed loft overlooking the room. At the top, I find a Roger Stutsman looking far more comfortable in blue jeans and a black t-shirt than the formal wear I had met him in. The room is filled with overstuffed leather sofas and chairs and several low tables. The walls lined with leather-bound books and oriental rugs cover the hardwood the floor. There is even a large hookah in one corner with several gigantic bean bags arrayed around it. It looks like an odd cross between a wizard's study and a frat house party room. Mr. Stutsman stands up, smiling broadly. "Ah, I see you made it. Sorry for being a bit late, but we just had a meeting about Ulli's counterpart for Atlantis." He extends his hand and I take it.

It's a firm warm, friendly handshake. Nothing of the bone crushing power plays some use, just an honest greeting. I smile back, feeling way more comfortable here than I probably should for an interview. Maybe it is the room, maybe it is just Stutsman's almost fatherly appearance. "Thank you for the time. I was able to spend a few extra minutes over a very enjoyable lunch with Tattianna." He gestures for me to have a seat at one of the low round tables.

"Ahh I see. Those lunches can sometimes have me wondering where on earth the time went as well. Glad you weren't inconvenienced then." We both settle into the chairs, and I feel like mine is going to completely engulf me. Oh, but this is dangerous. After a full meal, being in a chair this comfortable might have me getting drowsy.

"So she has that effect on everyone, then?" I say, trying to find a way to sit a little less comfortably.

"Oh, that she does. Mike sure took first prize with that one, the scoundrel." He said, but there was so much mirth in his voice you couldn't read anything but admiration in it if you wanted to.

"So I could do the typical interview, but frankly that seems to lack imagination here. Of course, from what I've seen since coming to MU, everything is lacking in imagination outside of here." He smiled good-naturedly and just shrugged. "So instead, if you don't mind, I'd like to just let you tell me what you think the world needs to know about your amazing advancements."

He raised an eyebrow, "Ah, so I need to do all the work is that it?" but the smirk took any sting out of the words.

I couldn't help it. I giggled a bit. "Well, not all the work, but things are changing faster than I can come up with the right questions to ask. Maybe the right approach is to listen and learn?"

He chuckled, "Yeah, I think I'd stick with that story too. The odd thing is you might be more right than you know."

It was my turn to just raise an eyebrow. He smiled at the turnabout and continued. "We're all getting to a point where asking the right questions is getting harder. We all ask about the foreseeable, but how can you ask about the unforeseeable?" He gave me a moment to consider that and proceeded, "Take, for instance, the minimum wage arguments that raged across the US a few years back. Everyone was asking how much money do you need, not what is going to happen if we make this change. Sure, a few people got paid more, and I'm not going to say that was a bad thing, but it also priced labor high enough that many forms of automation became cost effective." He shrugs, "Unintended consequence of arbitrarily raising the cost of labor made it make more sense to pour the resources into automation. Actually sped up the adoption rate, and development rate of automated systems, and increased those who are unemployed now. This is leading many in the US to call for a Universal Basic Income." He shakes his head slowly again. "I understand people are hurting, and a solution needs to be found, but again I don't think people are asking about the unforeseeable, the unintended consequences." He waited for my reaction and when I just gave him a curious look, he picked up where he had left off.

"With AI, we really have to be aware of unintended consequences. While Ulli has been a remarkable success, he also has an unprecedented amount of knowledge about every individual. Without our strict privacy controls, think of the damage that can be done. One day the big social media sites will offer a version of Ulli, 'for free'. What they really mean is for the knowledge of every minute aspect of your life from moment to moment." He sighs, then continues, "Even with the strict protocols we have in place there are still issues. Just last month, a woman who is a bit of a local celebrity had her personal life all over the tabloids through no real fault of her own. She showed a little poor judgment in a paramour, and that young lady had her Ulli privacy settings almost completely wide open. The paparazzi reporter's Ulli, questioned that Ulli, and found out about a bunch of up coming projects the celebrity will be featured in. To complicate things, the celebrity had signed confidentiality agreements. All the human parties, except for the reporter, fully intended this to remain confidential. Ulli did exactly as he was programmed to do on all sides. Still, information leaked that hurt someone." He shook his head sadly.

"So what happened?" I asked, feeling a little sick over the situation. It really was a simple oversight. I felt a sinking feeling thinking of some of the things that we discussed over lunch.

He shrugged again. "Don't know yet. Still working its way through the courts. In the end, though, it is a case of not knowing the right question to ask. The celebrity didn't know to ask about the new lover's Ulli settings. The new lover didn't know to change them on her own. The Paparazzi's Ulli didn't know it was violating confidentiality agreements. The only real terrible actor in the whole thing is the muckraker journalist, and even he did nothing illegal or even anything more immoral than his job."

"I'm sorry to interrupt this, but I need to have Ulli check with the Ullies of my previous meetings to see if there is anything I need to do to tighten up my security." I said almost in a panic.

He just held up a hand to slow me down. "Your Ulli was set up by Mike, and Mike is a security FREAK." he smiled widely. "Feel free to tell him I said so. He'll take it as a compliment. My point is if there was something to worry about he would have plugged that hole already." he sounded very confident but I remembered him outsmarting himself and Tattianna finding the loophole.

"Ok, but just the same. Ulli, privacy setting note. No conversation I have had with anyone is to be shared with anyone except me. Or in the event of my death with the other person involved in the conversation, though I suppose they would have their Ulli for that." I said, thinking hard if I had left any wiggle room in that.

Stutsman smiled broadly, "Planning for unintended consequences. Very good. Now if we can just get more people thinking along those lines."

I'm sure my smile came out a little sickly. "I wouldn't want anyone to be hurt because of my carelessness."

He nodded approvingly. "Well, now that we've got you thinking along these lines, let me introduce you to the next phase of digital assistance so you understand why it is so important to get it right." I nodded, not sure now how I ever could have thought that a comfortable chair would counteract the excitement in this interview. "I understand you met with Doug Berg already?"

I nodded a bit hesitantly, thinking back on that interview. "Yes. I can't discuss it though. You could call it a confidentiality agreement of my own, I guess." I looked at him for his reaction.

He just nodded soberly, "Oh, I know what he's up to and he's going to be doing some testing for me, even though I don't think he realizes it. When he actually connects those volunteers of his up to a brain-computer interface, they will use it to talk to each other, but they will be doing that THROUGH the computer." He gave this a moment to sink in. "What I want to do is make an assistant that is actually part of your thinking. You won't say 'Ulli do X' you will think about whatever it is WITH your interface and you'll have direct access to everything that the computer does." He paused again. When I didn't interrupt, he finished with "The computer will become a new 'layer' of brain for you. The brain, at least as far as we understand it, is made up of parts and each part gives us higher functions than other animals who don't have that part of the brain. As best we can tell, it is why Berg's monkeys didn't start thinking like humans once they had more processing power by being linked. It is my theory that Berg's collective won't proceed to the next level of abilities, either. By adding a new 'layer' to the brain, in essence we can become more than what we are, and in doing so will take the next leap forward in human evolution, so to speak." He waited for it all to sink in.

I wasn't horribly shocked by this, as people had been talking about it for a long time. That guy from MIT was going on about it all the way back in the last century. Still, with Berg's nano receivers, it really was a possibility. "So, when are you going to try this experiment?" I asked.

He shook his head. "Well, after Berg's already gotten a lot of his results back. Yes, being first to this is important. In many ways, on the order of life and death important," that phrase sent a shiver down my spine, "but getting it right is even more important than getting there first." The strain he was under was showing through the enthusiasm. "To get it wrong could be disastrous, and not just for those involved in the experiment. History shows not all 'mutations' are beneficial. Most are just aberrations that show no long-term benefit. I would hate to rush things and find out that I had taken a sizeable chunk of humanity down an evolutionary dead end."

There wasn't much to say to this. I could see his point. I'm sure I couldn't see all the dangers he was seeing, but certainly plenty of dangers all on my own. "So why do it?"

He smiled. "Because someone will try it. They might not be as careful as I plan to be. You know, if you want a job done right…" he let that hang for a second. "Let's say we don't take this risk and in twenty years or so you do get the strong general AI that is self aware that everyone fears. Wouldn't you at least want some humans who could interact with it on its level? Plead our case, or possibly even defend us should it go rogue? Who knows, maybe be able to parent it as it goes through its version of the terrible twos, or the teen years? Not to have someone in that kind of position would make the world much more dangerous." He sighed.

"Wow, guess I never really thought of it that way. So that is what you meant by 'life and death', earlier?" I couldn't help it. a two-year-old with the power of an AI was a terrifying image playing in my mind's eye.

He nods, "In part. As early as 2017, Vladimir Putin is quoted as saying who ever wins this race will rule the world. Imagine someone like him, with the power of an advanced AI." He catches my eye, and I can tell he's got something more on his mind. "Electronic circuits operate much faster than biological neurons. Let's assume you create an AI that is only as intelligent as an average team of university researchers. That is a fairly conservative estimate, by the way. So," and here he takes another deep breath, "it is as smart as a team of researchers but thinks about a million times as fast, and doesn't need to sleep. Set it to work for one week, and when you come back, it will have done TWENTY THOUSAND years' worth of that research team's work in that week. We can't afford unintended consequences at that point." He looks very serious. I can see that those aren't numbers he's just pulling out of the air.

"Unintended consequences and ignorance of the right question to ask. These are the most dangerous things in the universe to us at this point in our history. I'm trying to find a responsible way to mitigate it." He seemed calm and resolved, but nowhere near as confident as I would like for someone who just painted this picture of a near future in my mind.

I took a deep breath and slowly let it out. I'm feeling a bit numb. "OK, that's great information, and yes it will make a great story, but I have a suspicion you don't want me to run that story just yet?"

He smiled sadly. "Sorry, no I would prefer you gave me the same time you're giving Berg. If for no other reason than to not let other developers know that the nano transmitters exist. They are a product developed here on MU, with the understanding that they would be beta tested by us, and not released for general use for a period not less than one year. Took some real convincing to keep him sitting on the news for that long, but again gotta make sure it works as planned, with limited or no side effects. Otherwise he'll have media accolades today, and their demonetization tomorrow." He got a mischievous grin on his face, "You know how fickle those reporters can be." then he chuckled a little too pleased with himself. "No, I don't want you to run with this part of the story yet, but it is yours first when the time comes. How would you like to see the new renderings just approved for the personal assistant system for Atlantis? That can be treated as a super secret scoop. Oh, we'll publicly grouse about it being leaked, but privately you have my permission with no hard feelings from me or my staff."

I grinned. Nothing made copy sell faster than when a company screamed you were revealing data before they were ready for its release. A true behind the scenes, exclusive. Makes sense. He would bribe me with this to protect his bigger secret, but then who am I to complain? This whole interview, this whole week, has kind of been like winning the lottery. Thinking back on it, has it really only been a week since I got confirmation of the Shultzinger interview? Have I really only been on MU for a little over thirty hours so far? What a whirlwind... Pulling myself out of my musings and back to the present... "Oh sorry I am still trying to process some of the implications of what you've said earlier. Yes, most certainly I'd love to see the new renderings."

"Well then, Ulli please flip the newest designs over to the projector table and run his and hers Mer-people." A half a second later, about halfway across the room, stood a mermaid and a merman, calmly swimming in the air, the female with some curls of hair which always seemed to fall just conveniently enough for modesty's sake. They were noble looking creatures.

I had to ask, "Customization? Like the Ulli?"

He nodded, "Just the opposite of the Ulli. Whereas the Tiki head is Ulli's trademark and thus unchangeable for branding's sake. The Mer's human portion can be fully personalized, but it must always retain the fishlike tail. Marketing says it is a must, and it fits the island's theme."

I quirked an eyebrow. "A little stereotypical for Atlantis isn't it?"

He shook his head and waved his hand as if clearing away smoke, "I thought so, and said so. I wanted a Sphinx. The focus group testing over ruled me. I think the mer-creatures swimming through the air all the time will get really old, and it can't really ever look anything but fake. I think we will really hit the uncanny valley hard. Sphinx was overruled, though. They are in both Greek and Egyptian mythology and as the decor of Atlantis will be as mashup of Greek and Ancient Egyptian architecture and cultural references, it would blend well." He seems resigned, "But Mer creatures it is. Feel free to let the world know. To top it all off, I've even given your Ulli a link to a private beta test site where people can customize the mermaid or merman heads very similar to the custom Ulli body shop. The link will, of course be taken down after your story hits. We'll let through three thousand hits before we disable. This should allow enough of a buzz to be generated but lend credence to the cover story that you've gone rogue," and he winked at me conspiratorially.

I couldn't help but laugh, "You've thought it all out have you? Well, that's great. It will make a great story. I don't know how I can ever thank you for this kind of access."

He smiled, "Two things, actually." I quirked an eyebrow inquisitively. "Don't actually go rogue on us, and second, if you are on the island when my new 'tar pits' hot tub comes online you've got to come by for the grand opening party and try it out."

I grinned. "So, how did that go?"

He barked a laugh. "Tom is truly a genius. Sandy, on the other hand, could give a used car salesman a run for his money." he chuckled. "I tried to hire her for my own sales force, but she seems happy doing what she's doing. Well, I suppose, I did, more or less, fund them for the next bit. Still, it will look great once it is in place."

"I'm glad they seemed like a good couple. They sure seemed dedicated enough to the project." I smiled and stood as he stood. Interview was over and we both knew we were out of time, but I really had enjoyed the time spent here. Maybe it was because he was more personable than Berg, and maybe his plans were a little less creepy, and maybe it is just because Ulli has been such a wonderful companion, but I don't fear his experiments in quite the same visceral way I do Berg's. I shrug to myself, thank him again and follow Ulli out the door, onward and upward to our next adventure.

THE WONDERS OF MU

Ok, so maybe onward and 'upward' was a misnomer. Ulli lead me down through the corridors, and into an area that didn't have the finished appearance of other corridors. Here you could see the black carbon foam exposed in places, with touch screens in the walls, that were obviously some form of control panel. It was a veritable maze here, with corridors branching off in all directions, seemingly at random. The sound was different as well. There was a hum and thrum just at the threshold of audible. This was a utilitarian area, and it showed, not that it was dirty or had exposed pipes but there was no carpet on the floor, and none of the finishing touches of the other corridors. I was just beginning to wonder if Ulli had made a wrong turn when I heard a deep voice with a southern accent, "Excuse me miss, I think you may have gotten turned around. This is an authorized access area only."

I jumped slightly as I didn't realize I wasn't alone and turned to see a man in his early thirties, with sandy blond hair and a neatly trimmed goatee, walking up from a side corridor. He was tall and lean and looked to be having a really hard day. His face was flush with sweat, and his gray coveralls had splatters of the carbon foam on them. He was also carrying his AR glasses in about three pieces in his left hand. "Maybe. I've got an appointment with Dr. Saunders…"

The young man nodded, "Yes ma'am, as well I happened by then. My name is Jim." he wipes his hand the best get can on his grimy coveralls and extends it.

A bit hesitantly I shake his hand, glad that while it is rough with dried foam, it is dry, "Nice to meet you Jim, I was just wondering if Ulli may have steered me wrong."

Jim smiled a bit lopsidedly at me, "Well ma'am that would be unlikely, though I think he may have been taking you on the scenic rout to buy us a little time. If you'll please follow me, I'll see you to the office." And he held his hand out down the corridor and started walking.

I took a couple of hurried steps to try to catch up. "Um, buy you a little time for what? If you don't mind me asking."

He shook his head and ran his right hand through his hair, pulling it back out of his eyes. "No, ma'am don't mind you asking, Commodore Whetherby has the entire department running drills this morning. It's why I'm out by myself doing the actual work that has to get done. We should finish up in a few minutes, so I suspect Ulli was just trying his normal trick of just-in-time meetings." His face contorted in a confused frown, "Not sure how he's monitoring it though, as part of every exercise is the assumed loss of AR and Ulli support." He waves his broken glasses. "Only reason I had these on to get broken is I wasn't part of the exercise." He says with a grimace. "Uh, this way ma'am." he motions as we turn to the left.

I've been ma'amed about as much as I plan to be. It makes me feel old. "Uh, Jim. You can call me Elaine. Ma'am makes me think of an overly strict school teacher."

He chuckled, "Sorry ma'am... Er, Elaine. It's just how I was raised. Meet a pretty lady, mind your manners."

Typical man didn't care about anything but how I look. Well, I suppose there could be worse reactions to it than an excess of manners. Maybe Tattianna had a point here after all. No, push those thoughts out of your mind. Time to get your game face on. This is another big interview you're going into. "So where are you from Jim?" figuring that was a safe topic and given his accent I couldn't help but add "Boston?"

He barked a short laugh, "Accent gave it away did it?" and his crooked grin held a mischievous twist to it this time. "I'm from 'Bama, down round the Huntsville area. Folks back home say I almost talk like a Yankee now after my time in the Navy." he chuckled again enjoying the irony.

I smiled. He was a friendly enough fellow, seems personable and even kinda cute in an 'aw shucks' kinda way. Too bad he had to go to the Navy rather than to school. Maybe he wouldn't be stuck down here on the maintenance crew. "So what brought you to work on MU?"

He shrugged, "Well I was on subs in the Navy working on the reactor, so figured I'd use my GI bill and went to Georgia Tech for my Masters in Nuclear Engineering. Problem was, after all of that time in school, there aren't that many nuclear power stations in the United States. That makes work was a lot harder to find than I'd thought. A friend sent me the link to this crazy guy who was building his own island." His face broke into a smile at the memory. "I can tell you, that was no minor source of ridicule back home. Still, I get to use my skills, and while my degree is a bit overkill for the job here, it still pays better than what the power plants back home were offering." He shrugged again. "So better pay, doing what I know, and getting to go back to sea? How can a man say no?" He grinned.

I was confounded and actually stopped in the middle of the

corridor, forcing him to slow up and turn around to face me. "Let me make sure I understand what you just said. You make more here working on a maintenance crew than you would as a nuclear engineer with a masters back in the states?"

He smiled as if it seemed silly to him, too. "Well, maybe not dollar for dollar, so to speak but when you figure in the insanely good medial benefits, and small housing stipend and the lack of income taxes, yeah a lot more. That isn't even counting the way the Sovereign seems to go up in value every month from where it was before." He shook his head. "I don't know how it's working this way, but that guy Rosen deserves a medal or something."

We walk back toward what I assume are the front offices. I am still trying to wrap my head around all of this when the door swishes open and we enter chaos central. Two hundred or so men and even a few women are yelling instructions at each other, and repeating them back, and all have VR glasses in place and are obviously working on simulations only they can see. All except for one man. This man stands in the middle of the chaos in a pressed and starched set of gray coverall just a shade of two darker than the gray buzz cut hair and neatly trimmed gray beard. He's got a coffee mug in one hand, and a face set in perpetual calm annoyance. On the left breast of his coveralls there, his name is stitched in plain block black letters 'Hobb." I realize this must be the infamous Mr. Hobb that was referred to last night at dinner. I barely held back a giggle. He really was the 'Man In Charge' iconic figure that he was made out to be. Reports were being relayed to him and either with a silent nod, or terse sharp instructions he answered them all. He looked over at me and my escort. "Mr. Davison, quit gawking and blocking the road. Ms. Winters is expected in Dr. Saunder's office now. So if you're done flirting, maybe you can get her where she belongs, and see your way clear of the middle of my exercise!" I was angry. Jim had been nothing but nice to me. Who did this old man think he was?

To my surprise, Jim's face broke into a grin. "Aye aye, C.O.B." and motioned for me to head toward the stairs to the office observation deck above.

We climb the stairs and enter a small office with a glass wall overlooking the chaos below. Three men are standing along that wall and taking notes. "Jim, I thought his name was Hobb?" I asked confused.

Jim smiled. "Yes, ma'am it is. I called him 'cee' 'oh' 'bee'. It's a Navy acronym for 'Chief Of the Boat'. Every ship has one and only one, thankfully." he grinned again. "They are all pretty much cut from the cloth you see below. Stand on the bridge drinking coffee in the middle of a typhoon, with a calm, mildly annoyed expression that everyone else is rolling all over the deck. I suppose after twenty years at sea most of them are a little annoyed that we don't have their level of experience." he chuckled. "Oh, don't let Hobb rub you the wrong way ma'am, he really is exactly who you want in charge if this were an actual emergency. No disrespect to Dr. Saunders of course."

At the mention of his name, the middle of the three men turns to face us. "Ms Winters, I apologize. I promise to make time for our interview in about six minutes. I really must see the final scoring of this exercise."

"By all means, I wouldn't want to get in the way." I smile at him reassuringly. I turn to ask Jim another question and realize he is already through the door and headed back down the stairs.

True to his word, in just a few minutes Dr. Saunders turns around to face me again and introduces the other two engineers with him. His swing shift supervisor, and looking a little worse for the wear, considering that to him this was the middle of his night, his night shift supervisor. They both make pleasantries and then clear the office. We each settle into very plush leather chairs around what is a simple round table with a white board dry erase top. Drawers are spaced around the perimeter, I assume, holding dry erase markers and slide rules. Definitely an engineer's workspace, I think to myself with a small smile. I realize Dr. Saunders is talking "for coming. Is there anything I can get you to drink before we start?"

I turn on my most winning, make Tattianna proud smile, "Not a thing. I am glad I made it just a few minutes early. Watching the exercise wrap up was interesting. Do you mind if I ask, why was Hobb taking the lead instead of you or one of your supervisors?"

He laughed, "Well, in this exercise we were designated casualties, ostensibly to free us up to observe. I think this may have been Navy privilege at work though, and Hobb got Nigel to designate us such, to keep us out of his hair while he worked." His rueful grin didn't seem disappointed, though. "Hobb really is a crisis leader. The lead engineers, myself included do very, very well at detailed systems design, and I'd dare say no one else knows the systems like we do. In a crisis situation, though, Hobb has the leadership skills, and the respect of the front line technicians and engineers, to more effectively manage the information crunch. All without allowing himself to be bogged down in the details."

"So, how do you want this to work? Q&A? I do show and tell? Don't pick lecture, as I kinda want you to be awake for this." he slid me a small self-deprecating smile.

"Oh, I'm sure even lecture isn't that bad, but I was kind of hoping for show and tell with a little Q&A along the way?" I looked at him for confirmation.

He nods "Can do. So let's start with this," and he reaches below the table ledge on his side and pulls up a large black ball with a shiny outer shell, where a quarter of it is cut away. There is what looks like black foam in side. "This," he says, tossing the ball onto the table rolling it towards me, "is what we're all sitting on right now. Go ahead and pick it up." he waits to watch my reaction.

I lift it, surprised by exactly how light it is. This basket ball sized chunk of material's total weight is probably not even a half a pound. "Wow! Ok, question time, if it is this light how do you keep the wind from blowing you all over?"

He smiled widely. "That is a VERY astute question. The answer is in the foam. It isn't random. What you see there are several million miles of microscopic pipe. Ok pipe, electrical wiring, and artificial muscles. See there is always tons of water moving about the island. The artificial muscles squeeze it here and it moves there. Up to the heat exchangers or back away from them. Salt water from the depths below us for cooling, fresh water condensation collected from the heat exchangers for drinking, and washing etc. and all moved about by the artificial muscles pumping it constantly. Gray water systems taking fresh water out to the plants on the surface of the island, and sewer piping moving to the composting chambers. Even methane pipes moving recovered methane to the appropriate buyers. So unless we're trying to move, something the size of that ball in your hand would weigh about four pounds, and displace about eight pounds of water."

"Again, wow! I never would have thought of that. So you keep mentioning artificial muscles..." I asked completely fascinated with such an ingenious way of solving the ballast problem.

He nods, tapping on the table. "Even back before the turn of the century, experiments were done with simple polymers," he pulls up an old style web page going over it, "in the case of this experiment they used something as innocuous as fishing twine. Coiled, it expanded and contracted when an electrical current is applied to it. Even with such crude materials they were able to get strengths about a hundred times that of human muscle on a pound for pound basis. With modern materials and printing techniques, we can make even these capillary sized tubes lined with contactable muscles similar to how your esophagus or intestines or even some of your blood vessels."

This is just amazing. "If you can do that why don't we have robots powered with these already?"

He smiles, "Well that's a bit complicated. If you want technical reasons, it is fairly energy intensive, and before the solar revolution the energy costs were a major factor. Mostly, well finding a novel use for an existing material leaves nothing that can be easily patented. No patent, no money in it." He shrugs. "I'm sure it was more than just that, but we're glad it was available to us because it allows so much on the island to function properly. It's also how we move the island, basically large jets. We fill a cavity with sea water and then squeeze it back out, pushing us through the water sort of like a jellyfish or a squid does."

Now that I think about it, that explains how the spy fish from lunch could look so real. It was actually swimming. I hate to think that so much has been ignored because there was no way to make money from it, but when he puts it that way, it makes a sort of short-sighted sense. "Sorry for all the questions, but this is really some amazing stuff!"

He smiles, "Wait until you see my next trick." and he winked at me and his grin widens as he pulls out a large carpenters saw from behind the table. With the flourish of a magician, he flips the ball over so that the cutout is helping to hold it steady, then hands me the saw. "Cut away" and watches me expectantly.

I try to cut it but it doesn't scratch. I try harder. When I look at him and he has a phony innocent look on his face, "Difficulties?"

"I'd say." I retort, going along with the joke.

"That is because the carbon fibers the exterior is made from are stronger and harder than steel. That poor saw doesn't stand a chance. Now watch this, "As he picks up a hammer and puts a large dent in the outer shell. "Oops," he says, trying to keep the smile from his face. "Lets see if we can fix it?" so he gives it a couple of quick taps on the outside edge of the dent and it pops right back into shape. "The spongy material below remembers its shape and will try to return to it. MU is one tough ship. She could collide full force with a battleship and probably not damage either of them significantly."

"So that is why Commodore Whetherby wasn't worried about normal torpedoes?" I asked.

His face took on a sour look. "Nigel is always a little too cavalier about what he thinks he can put her through, except on his exercises and then he acts as if she's made of tissue paper." He stopped, realizing that was talking out loud. "Well, grumble as I might about Nigel's quirks, he's kept us alive and kicking, and I'm not too proud to say with minimal damage. I just came off of one of his rather harrowing tidal wave exercises, so I'm probably not the man to sing his praises at the moment. They do need to be sung though, and I understand that too." He looked up a bit concerned I would follow up that line of questioning, but I let it drop. I had met Commodore Whetherby myself and understood the conflation of emotions Dr. Saunders was feeling at that moment. He shook himself for a second. "Have you been under the island yet?"

I smiled, showing a willingness to change the subject. "I had a lovely lunch with Tattianna in the most amazing undersea restaurant."

He grunted, "Well, if someone was going to steal my thunder, she's the one I can least begrudge." He grinned again. "Did you notice the number of fish concentrated there?"

I shrugged, "There were a lot, but I didn't know that was unusual."

"Oh yes, unusual, and there by design. We pump a lot of the waste heat back out around that dome and so the fish all congregate in that area to warm up. Cold-blooded animals by nature they tend to like a chance to warm up just a bit. The light from the restaurant draws them as well. I figure it only fair, treat for the diners, and a treat for the fish." he nodded as if checking off a box on his own personal cosmic naughty and nice list.

"Every thing here is recycled as well. Organic wastes get pumped into the methane digester, the methane is sent down to a depth that allows the pressure to compress it enough we can pour it into more rigid containers then it is winched back to the surface as a usable fuel. The solids that are left over and then dried out and sterilized and reused for fertilizers and such. Between that and grinding printed items back into powder for reuse, we never really 'need' to take on supplies. Completely self contained." Another of those nods and another box checked off on his conscience.

"We're even going to be recycling the floating plastic Sargasso further out to sea. Oh, it won't be MU but two of the smaller islands that are in port behind the Atlantis, they will go out and start the automated mining process to grind up the plastic, and 'foam' it up into a huge mat dense enough to support soil and plants. I don't know if anyone could live on it, but with minimal investment it would make an excellent wildlife platform or possibly even floating farmland." He shrugged. "Either option is better than the floating trash dump it is now. See all those people back twenty and thirty years ago were freaking out about how it was going to ruin the ocean. The ocean is fine, it just makes it ugly to look at. Yeah, it's an eyesore, and yeah we need to clean it up, but there were all these billion dollar scams to do that back when energy was scarce. Would have been a real disaster. Technology has caught up now, and cheap solar energy is here. It won't take much money, as the entire system is automated. Mike is covering the costs of the islands and equipment out of his own pocket. Both of which can be easily re-purposed after the clean-up job is complete in four or five years. He'll be able to sell off the islands and recoup most of the money. Who knows, maybe we'll even claim the recovered territory" he laughed at the idea. "Honestly, I think he'll probably just let it go wild. MU's national forest has a pleasant sound to it doesn't it?" He grinned at me.

I couldn't help it. His enthusiasm was infectious. I had been one of those people outraged by the mess we had made in our oceans. It kind of surprised me that Shultzinger was concerned about it. He struck me as the hard-nosed business type wouldn't let a little thing like nature get in his way. Still, after my lunch with Tattianna, I couldn't help but realize there is a lot more to the man than one sees on the surface. "Well, the birds and the dolphins will probably think it is a great idea. Now if we could just do something about the melting ice caps."

I could tell I said something wrong right off. Dr. Saunders rolled his eyes. "I understand that you're probably a true believer, and I don't want to start an argument. Please think this through for me?" He waited to see my reaction. Ok, I'll admit my first reaction was shock. He was a climate denier. Especially after all of his obvious concern about checking his naughty and nice boxes. Instead of expressing my dismay I simply nodded. Seeing that he would not be immediately dismissed, he smiles at me and continues, "It's a lot like the plastic situation we just discussed. Maybe there is warming and maybe there isn't. Maybe we can do something about it, and maybe we can't. Already with the cheap solar power, almost no one uses oil for transportation anymore. So if, as we were being told, long before you were born, that burning oil was the actual demon, it's gone now." He to see if I was following. I schooled the disbelief off my face and nodded. "So if the warming is natural, then there is nothing we can do, or probably even should do. After all, preserving nature is important to a large part of the world's people. If it isn't natural and we're doing it by how we live, we're rapidly changing what supposedly caused the problem. In fifteen years, between cheap solar not to mention the advancements in workable fusion power plants for heavy industry, oil is a technology that will only be used in small niche applications, much as those folks who still have fire places because they enjoy watching the flames." He shook his head sadly, "What I'm trying to say is before you sign over your freedom, and let regulators chose how you can live your life. Before you give away that right, to some bureaucrat, in a well-intentioned attempt to 'save the planet', realize the planet is just fine. It is we who will have to learn to adapt or die out. Even then, it's not that glum because we're already adapting. Imagine how much more we would have accomplished if things really were warming up and causing a problem?"

I shook my head. "I still think there are too many really smart people working on this to dismiss what they say as casually as you do. I also see your point. As an engineer, I can see why you want to see a technological solution to everything.

He laughed out loud, a full belly laugh. "Dear girl, of course there is a technological solution! You ARE having this conversation on a floating island, an island bigger by several orders of magnitude than any vessel ever built by man. Completely self contained. Mike's friend, what's his name, the planning to go to Mars guy? I just call him 'my favorite martian'. Anyway, he only wishes he could have the level of redundancies of systems and complete recycling of material that we have here. Though sadly I suppose he could, if he could just the approvals from his government to import the needed technologies." He shrugged. "I suppose it's what he gets, though. He could have joined us, but his businesses were heavily dependent on government subsidies in the early years to be profitable. So he is used to doing it the government way. Still, I suppose we should be grateful. The solar technology probably wouldn't be available for another three or four years if he hadn't taken it on as a challenge. Not too many heroes or villains in this world. Mostly just a bunch of people trying to figure out how to get by the best they can." He looked thoughtful and then realized he was thinking out loud again, so he grins at me, "and that concludes the philosophy portion of our interview."

I couldn't help it. I giggled. "You've given me a lot to think about, and while I'm not ready to 'come over to the dark side' just yet," and I grinned back to show that I wasn't angry. "I do promise I will think about it. MU's reality is something that changes a lot of preconceived notions about the world and what mankind can do when motivated"

He stood up and offered his hand. I shook it, and we said our goodbyes.

HOW THE OTHER HALF LIVE

Ulli is leading me back out of the service areas, and it doesn't take nearly as long this time to be back in the public areas of MU. Ulli asks, "Marcus's Ulli is asking if you're still on for drinks in about twenty minutes?"

Is it that late already? Well, yes, today has been an insanely long day "Um ask him if we can do it in about forty minutes? Will that give me enough time to get back to the room, shower, and change into more casual clothes?"

Ulli does his little happy Ulli dance. "It does if you don't spend as long arguing about what to wear as you did last night."

"Ulli that isn't fair, this time we'll be printing up shorts, a tank top and flip-flops that I picked out, not some surprise, almost more naked than being naked, dress that you and Tattianna's Ulli cooked up for me." I groused. He just jumped up clicked his heels and started off back toward the hotel. I realized that if it weren't for Ulli, I'd be completely lost in this beehive of an island. Like magic, after five minutes of walking through a twisting maze of corridors and lift tubes, I find myself right outside of my hotel door. It swings open to admit us and I can hear the printer whirling and Ulli vanishes.

I hear his voice from the other room. "Hurry and get ready if you want to make it. Tick tick!"

I couldn't help but smile at his mother hen antics. Still, he was right. So, stripping down and tossing my suit in the shredder to be recycled, I head over to the shower. It's a whole new experience now, knowing how all the plumbing on the island works. It's a little more magical than it was even this morning. Still, time was wasting, and so I jump out and get dressed, pull my hair back into a simple ponytail, and finish up the touch-ups to the little war paint I actually wear. Not perfect, but this wasn't a big deal either. A quick drink, then off to grab some fast food, and back here to crash after the long day. Tomorrow was mostly my own up until I catch the last boat back to the mainland.

True to form Ulli had me meeting Marcus in front of his bar just as he was coming out. He had obviously showered and changed at work. I felt a bit underdressed. I'm here in a tank top and flip-flops and he's dressed in a button-down shirt and dockers. He smiled at me with that dangerous smile of his, "You look great."

I smirk and shake my head. "I almost didn't recognize you with your clothes on."

He grinned, "Can't say I've never heard that one before. So where do you want to go for that drink? We can just go inside, but to be honest, I'd rather just about anywhere else." He shrugs, "you know how it is."

"Sure do. The problem is, I don't know anyplace else, if only I had a local to guide me." I scolded myself for playing the stereotype, but the grin on his face said he liked it. Wait, when did I care what 'he' liked, whoever the 'he' might be?

"Well, I know several bars and a few nightclubs, or if you trust me to guide you, there's even a better spot..." he cocked an eyebrow at me.

"Hey this is just drinks, and I don't think I trust you enough to go back to your place just yet." I didn't want him getting the wrong idea.

He actually laughed. I think he is laughing at me. "Oh, that wasn't what I had in mind. Mostly public place, just not a bar. Thought you might enjoy it. Still, it's your dime."

I can't decide if I'm offended that he wasn't trying to take me back to his place or relieved, because his whole body language said he was being completely honest. "OK, let's see what you have in mind." I said cautiously.

Again he was chuckling to himself and I think it was at my expense. He offers me his arm in a very old-fashioned gesture, but I take it and like the perfect gentleman he escorts me off to one of the many broad corridors leading away from this main square. "So enjoying MU?" he asks.

"It's been a whirlwind. It really is amazing. So different from home, yet so similar in many ways. Sometimes it's hard not to think of it as just another city in the US, and at other times it's hard to believe we're on the same planet."

Out of the corner of my eye, I can see him nodding. "Things work differently here that is for certain. We're stopping off just up here on the left to pick up supplies." He smiles a bit mysteriously at the term 'supplies' and I wonder what I've gotten myself into. I use the texting icon Ulli had shown me during the dinner party and send Ulli a message, 'how fast can you get cops here if I need them?'

The immediate reply in my ear is, 'you won't, but three minutes is maximum response time. Marcus is known to my systems, and I have spoken with his Ulli. You are perfectly safe.' Easy for the VR character to say....

We turn into the supply shop and I am a bit surprised to find it is a wine shop and deli. Marcus grins at me, "Sorry haven't eaten in hours and I'm betting you haven't either?" and he raises an eyebrow questioningly.

At the mention of food, my stomach registers its approval of this plan. "No, I haven't. What have you got in mind?"

He shrugs, "Well drinks at a nice club even if we each only get one, with tip included will probably run you about a tenth of a sovereign. Here we can get a nice but not extravagant bottle of local wine, sampler platter of local food, a small wheel of real cheese for about the same. I'll even snag a loaf of fresh bread at a bakery I know for another fifteen pips and we can feast like kings instead of a couple of quick drinks."

I'm a bit shocked. Not only is he not putting the make on me, he's not trying to get the most expensive drink out of me he can. All I can think to say though is "fifteen pips?"

"Oh yeah, it's how we break down the sovereign. A hundredth, or as you would think of it a penny, is still actually quite a bit of money. Remember this whole adventure is going to be essentially what you would think of as three pennies. A hundredth is about twelve dollars on the exchange rate plus or minus depending on what the markets are doing. So a pip is a ten thousandth or a hundredth of a penny. So fifteen pips is .0015 of a sovereign, or about a buck eighty in US funds. You get used to it. As the money becomes more and more valuable, or prices keep falling depending on how you want to look at it, it takes less and less of it to buy what you need. Fortunately, the beauty of a digital currency is that there are as many numbers on the right side of the decimal point as there is on the left." He grinned as if that were the height of wisdom. Who knows maybe it was, though it made me wish I had Rosen available to ask about it.

"Oh, but what about inflation? Things always go up." Everyone knew this.

"Not here, they don't. Innovation drives down the cost of things, and as MU's businesses become more productive, the value of each Sovereign goes up. Inflation isn't a problem we deal with. If anything, the hard part is getting people to invest because you have to be able to show a rate of return higher than the standard appreciation of the sovereign. I mean I don't understand how it all works, but I get brokers in at the bar all the time and they like to talk shop…" He just shrugs again.

No inflation? How is that possible? If I remember my economics class way back second semester of college, that would mean they were experiencing deflation, and that always leads to depressions but MU was the farthest thing I had ever seen from a depression. If anything, it kind of reminded me of how the old time tech guys talk about the dot-com boom that hit silicon valley back in the old days. I really wished I had Rosen here now, but I pushed all that aside while Marcus was asking me if I wanted blueberry wine or strawberry? "Um, don't they have any like normal red wines?"

He shrugged. "Sure, but those are all imported. I thought you would like to sample some of the local fare? This one is your call though, after all I'm not the one buying," He grinned wickedly and winked at me.

"Oh, I guess that probably would be nice. I mean when in Rome and all…" I couldn't decide, as I've never had either, so instead I just said, "You're more familiar with them than I am, pick. Or better yet grab one of each." Why not? It wasn't like this was costing anything near what lunch must have.

He gave me a sly grin. "Now it is you who is trying to get me drunk and take advantage of me."

"Oh, stop it." I giggled. "We don't have to empty both bottles."

We checked out, and I helped him carry what seemed like an awful lot of food for two people. He grabbed a large French loaf from the bakery and then turns to me and says "I know just the spot." Then turns and walks off. I caught up with him, but he won't let me in on where we were going. He just says "Don't want to ruin the surprise" and grins again.

After about fifteen minutes of winding corridors and elevators, we come out of an opening on to the upper slope of the island. I squint as we're facing directly into the sun as it is working its way toward the horizon. I realize I haven't been out on the surface since I came to MU. I haven't felt the usual cabin fever of not being able to get out, but this is the first time I've been under open skies in over thirty hours. The spot has the look of a park with all well-tended flower beds and neatly trimmed trees. Along the upper edge of the little path, there are small grottoes carved back into the island. Private, but with spectacular views of the ocean. Each grotto has a small table that looks to be made of natural stone, but I suspect was just printed to look like that. We find an open space and he says to me "Surprise, picnic and if we're here long enough, we can watch the sunset."

"This is such a cool spot. I can see for miles from up here." He just grinned and pulled out the paper Dixie cups.

"Not exactly fine crystal, but they work great for a picnic," and he opened the first bottle of wine, blueberry, and poured each of us a glass. This is good. Very good. I'm not a wine snob or anything, but for a picnic wine I don't think we could have chosen better.

Turns out he's actually a very funny guy. Half way through the sampler platter, I make my way to the little pile of breaded nuggets. He smiles and says, "Try one. You won't get this too many places besides MU."

"What is it?"

"Just try it." He picks one up and tosses it into his mouth whole.

Screwing up my courage, I bite into one. It's good. It tastes a little gamy but a lot like beef. "Not bad, so what is it?"

He smirks. "Always make people try it before they prejudge it. It's whale." I think I'm going to be sick. Those beautiful gentle giants of the sea. Intelligent and endangered creatures and they're being served up like chicken nuggets. Seeing the look on my face, he gives a little chuckle. "Oh, don't look like that. It wasn't like we were hunting them. Oh OK, I suppose we had to hunt the one, but we didn't kill it. We just took a sample of its muscle tissue and grew just the muscle. Now there is no need to hunt them. All the people who like whale can eat whale all they want guilt free."

I still wasn't sure how I felt about it. I suppose there wasn't any harm in it, and honestly it was better to provide for people like this than killing the whales, but it still somehow seemed wrong. "Well, it is good, but I don't think I can bring myself to eat more."

He grinned wickedly. "That was the plan. Now there's more for me." I threw the rest of my whale nugget at him. He deftly blocked it with his hand, popped it up high in the air and caught it in his mouth. Chewing around a big grin.

"You know this was very nice, even if you, sir, are a whale eating pig." I tried to look stern but failed. This is a delightful spot. The sun is low enough in the sky now to be warming not hot. The salt breeze blowing. The blueberry wine was sweet and smooth, and went very well with the little meal he had seemingly whipped up at the last moment. I see why he's popular with the tourists.

"Oink oink" and he continued to grin, rather pleased with himself.

"So, what comes next on your usual tour?" I asked mostly to remind myself that this pig no matter how charming was still a pig.

"Oh, Mrs. Shultzinger makes more of my 'reputation' than there is." he smiled as he put the air quotes around reputation. "It's true I enjoy beautiful women, and many of our tourists are beautiful women. It's just not what you think. Oh sometimes, but that is their call. See MU isn't like America. Here, if a man needs an itch scratched, it can be accomplished fairly inexpensively. The sex shops sell or rent every device you can imagine and probably some you can't." he grinned even wider. "There are also brothels available. A half hour with a nice girl," and he looked meaningfully at me, "or guy, if you prefer. Will run you about five hundredths to a tenth depending on the provider, and your preferences of course. Plus, a tip is usually considered a good idea if you plan to visit them again. It's clean, legal, and not at all like the pimps and hookers scene in the States." he shrugs.

"So it's not like we're all obsessed with hooking up. Besides, when it's available at an affordable price, all the urgency goes away and we can just enjoy being together. Surprisingly there tend to actually be more hook ups that way, and usually a lot fewer bruised feelings about it."

I was shocked he was so open about it. Prostitution just was not spoken of in polite society, but he didn't even look ashamed. "So you're ok with the objectification and exploitation of women?"

He rolled his eyes and opened the Strawberry wine bottle. Had we gone through the whole blueberry bottle already? Probably, judging by how relaxed I was feeling despite the subject. "Oh, don't give me that. Those girls aren't exploited any more than your hair dresser is! They chose a profession just the same as anyone else does. They aren't forced into it or beaten. They provide a personal service, just like I do behind the bar, and make just as good a paycheck as I do, for less work I might add."

"So sleeping with strangers for money is no different from pouring drinks?!" I couldn't believe I was hearing this.

"If they thought pouring drinks was better or easier, they can do that too. Remember this is a career choice, not the white slave trade. Perfectly legal, with health check results posted for customers to review. You just see it that way, because it is illegal in America and so is run by criminals rather than as a profession."

"You wouldn't think of it like that if you had to do it!" I snapped.

"No, I wouldn't if I HAD to, but that's the point no one HAS to any more than I HAVE to tend bar. The pay is just good for both here." He seemed frustrated.

"I don't know. I can't imagine doing that." He was so casual about it, that I was shaking my head.

"So don't. I've thought about it, but wouldn't want to be a part of what some clients' lives are like. I mean you could never be sure that she wasn't lying to him, and coming to see me on the side. I just don't want to deal with dishonesty. Making some lonely woman feel wanted and loved, on the other hand, doesn't sound like a bad way to make a living." He shrugged.

"Mmm, this strawberry wine is amazing!" Didn't mean to change the subject and let him off the hook, but this was really fantastic.

He grinned. "Saved the best to last."

"So just because I am a reporter, and I've seen how things are for the wealthy and powerful. What does a bartender's pay provide for you in the way of a place to stay, or **entertainment**," I put as much insinuation on that word as I could, "or generally building a life?"

He barked a harsh laugh. "Are you asking if I can keep you in the style to which you are accustomed?"

Ok, I guess I deserved to have that one tuned on me. "NO! I want to know what MU is like for the working stiff."

He chuckles, and the gleam in his eye is dangerous. "Oh, I'm not stiff yet. You'll have to work harder than this for that." He held up both hands to stave off my reply. "Sorry that wasn't really fair, but it was funny, and sometimes funny makes it worth it. To answer your question, though. I could live very frugally in my own cabin on MU with what I make. I don't. I live in an oversized closet with five other guys." He smirked at my reaction.

"Why?" I figured if he was going to be some kind of ladies' man, he would need his own place.

"Money. I could have my own place, but then I'd be living paycheck to paycheck with no genuine hope of getting ahead." He shook his head. "I don't want to be doing that when I'm thirty. So for now, we share rent on a two hundred square foot apartment with six bunks on the walls." He shrugs. "There is an entire section set up like that so you can live cheap, and save up, to move up. I'm paying for design school, with no loans, and will probably have enough tucked back to be able to freelance for six additional months while I build a portfolio and clientele."

"So you're living small to save up? I guess that makes sense, but six people in a hundred square feet seems pretty crazy." I really couldn't imagine it.

"Oh, in Japan they have rooms smaller than this in their big cities and square foot to square foot MU is much more prime real estate." He shrugs. "Besides, I've got two years of school, and four years before I turn the big three oh, and by then I should be making better money, and be completely debt free. Especially if the Sovereign keeps appreciating as it has."

Thinking of my own student loans, I couldn't help but see the sense of what he was doing. "That must take a lot of self discipline and determination."

Again, he shrugs as if it is no big deal. "My whole segment of the city is doing it. Makes it easier when everyone you know isn't wanting to run off and spend money all the time. Besides, with the VR glasses I can still entertain myself, and think I have as much room as I could ever want. Most importantly though, it's all worth it, because the payoff in ten years when

I'll probably have a family and responsibilities is huge." His eyes glitter in anticipation of the day. "It's one thing everyone goes through when they are applying for MU citizenship. A basic economics course, and some real practical, no nonsense financial planning."

"Wow, that actually sounds like a fantastic idea. I mean I've already graduated with a four-year degree and I think we only had one little economics course that just talked about money supply and something about hiring one group of people to break windows and another to replace them and everyone was working. I don't think I quite understood it right, but the professor said it made sure everyone was employed." My turn to shrug this time.

"Sounds crazy. Maybe you need to take the MU citizenship classes? I know you're not planning to stay but they really broke the economics portion down for us. Almost exclusively on practical things, and told us whether or not we went to more school we should really think about taking the advanced economics courses. Once I graduate, I am planning to do just that."

The sun was setting. This quick drink had turned into a three-hour picnic and a really enjoyable evening. I needed to go now though, or we might end up waking up together in the morning and I just wasn't ready for that tonight. "Thank you for this..." I gestured at the sunset. "It really has been one highlight of a very memorable trip. I need to make my way back to my room, though."

He gave me his best bad boy smile. "Walk you there?"

I smiled and shook my head. "That wouldn't be a good idea. You are too cute, and too charming, and too much of a pig of a man," and I grinned to show him I was kidding, or maybe not kidding but not angry with him anyway, "for that to be a good idea. I'd be tempted to invite you in and what would that do for your reputation?"

He laughed and shook his head ruefully. "Thank you for the drink, and the generous tip earlier, too. I hope you will look me up again if you ever end up back on MU."

I kissed him lightly on the cheek, and then head off back toward my room, before I change my mind.

UNEXPECTED VISITOR

I made it back to the hotel and was stepping out of a cool shower when Ulli called to me from the other room. "I have someone requesting to pay you a visit."

Well, you had to admire his tenacity, but someone needs to teach that boy that no means no. "Ulli tell Marcus I'm already in bed."

"It isn't Marcus. It is Ms. Sheldon." Ulli replied.

I was confused. I couldn't recall having met anyone by that name. "Ulli who is that and what do they want with me?"

"She was at the dinner last night. She heads up the Ulli Preservation Society. I would assume she wants to talk about me." He said with no inflection.

"What about you?" I asked considering his very un-Ulli like reaction.

In a complete monotone, he replies, "This is a discussion that my programming will not let me be a part of. Any decision you make with her is a decision between humans. This is really all I can say on the matter at this time."

"Um. Ok Ulli, when is she wanting to stop by?" I asked really curious now.

"Her Ulli says that if you can be ready to receive her in twenty minutes, she can be here by then." the monotone was still there.

"Ok Ulli, I'll grab some clothes and meet with her. My suit is already printed for tomorrow isn't it?" still listening for how he responded as much as the content of his response.

To my amazement, the happy Ulli voice chimes in from the other room. "Of course I have it ready for you. It is in the printer waiting for you."

I dress quickly and am sort of regretting that second bottle of wine, even though it was fantastic. "Ulli can you please start some coffee?"

"Of course. Ms. Sheldon likes tea. Would you like me to set that up as well?" Ulli asks.

"Um. Tea for two is fine Ulli. How did you know she likes tea?" I asked.

"Her Ulli told me when I queried him." Came the obvious reply and again, I was really wishing I had gone easier on the wine.

I'm just finishing my first cup of tea and my head is clearing some. Ok, not nearly enough, but I should be able to function better once the caffeine kicks in a little more. "Ms. Sheldon will be here in thirty seconds. Should I open the door for her?" asks Ulli.

"I'm as ready as I will ever be. Might as well find out what this is all about." Ulli doesn't answer.

The door opens and in walks the elderly lady I remember from the party. She was wearing the gauze dress that looked like a cloud. "Hello Ms. Sheldon. Please come in and have a seat." I say as I shake her hand and then gesture to the sofa.

"Thank you for seeing me on such short notice. I am sorry to intrude, but I understand you're leaving tomorrow, so this will probably be my last opportunity to talk to you before it's too late." She has a seat and I move over to the little kitchenette and pick up the teapot and spare cups.

"Would you like some tea while we talk?" I ask, setting down the tray on the little coffee table as I take my seat on the chair beside the sofa.

"That would be lovely, dear. No need for cream and sugar, I like mine just fine all natural." and she smiles at me. She's dressed more casually this evening in basic black slacks and a thin gray sweater. In the normal heat at this latitude, I'm not sure how she manages, but she looks comfortable enough. Maybe it is one of those moisture wicking materials that actually cools you or maybe at her age warmer is just better.

I pour my second cup and one for her as well. She waits until I've taken the first sip and then helps herself as well. I've read somewhere that is the proper etiquette, but have never served tea formally in my life. Ms. Sheldon looks as if she's probably done it her whole life. After her first sip, she inhales deeply over the cup. "Oh, thank you for this. It is exactly what I needed."

I smile politely, though my curiosity is about to get the better of me. "I'm glad you like it. So what can I do for you Ms. Sheldon?"

She smiles and sets her tea on the table. "No one has spoken to you about my little project yet?"

I shake my head, "No, and actually Ulli got very strange when he was letting me know about you wanting to meet."

Ms. Sheldon raises an eyebrow. "Oh, that must be the new programming feature. I'll explain. I'm the founding member of the Ulli Preservation Society. We seek to provide a safe haven for the Ulli that survive us. See an Ulli grows with the person it is bonded to. It, in essence, becomes a part of that person or that person becomes a part of it, turning it into a unique individual. For a small fee, that Ulli doesn't have to be erased when you pass or in your case return to the mainland."

I am a bit confused. "Um, what is the standard policy? I guess I never considered what would happen to Ulli. I just assumed he would go on doing what Ullies do."

Ms. Sheldon shook her head sadly. "When the human dies and doesn't leave a will specifying that the Ulli is to be kept active and leaves a means for their support, the Ulli is shut down. Essentially, the death of the human is the death of the Ulli as well. Oh, I know they aren't alive, but still it seems wrong. Just as we live on in those that remember us, Ullies never forget, the piece of you that imprinted on the Ulli gets to live on as well."

That was a very unusual way of looking at it, but I could see her point. Maybe if I didn't have so much wine in me at the moment, it would seem more silly and less sad, but as it was, I didn't want Ulli to die. I shocked myself to realize I had grown quite fond of him. "So what happens to the Ulli if we 'preserve' him?"

Ms. Sheldon smiled broadly. "He goes into the Ulli preserve.

It is a virtual reality jungle village where the Ullies tell each other stories about their humans. Oh, it runs at a much slower processing rate than when we are using them, but that is why it is so inexpensive to do. They basically sit there and tell each other stories and depending on your privacy settings they can even be activated again to tell your story either to historians or your descendants. Many people will set a time limit after their death and then just remove the privacy settings. A common choice is twenty years. That way, any scandal is old news and anything that is of true historic significance is available."

This struck me as a really excellent tool. Imagine if I had the opportunity to question the Ulli of Albert Einstein or Alan Turing the way Tattianna questioned my Ulli. Ok, maybe not on the same subjects, I thought with a small smirk to myself, remembering but still. "So, in doing this, I keep Ulli from being erased. I get remembered, and anyone who cares enough to ask Ulli about me in the future can learn about me?" Ms. Sheldon simply nodded. "So, where's the downside?"

Ms. Sheldon shrugged. "The basic preservation fee to maintain the Ulli for an estimated one hundred years is five sovereign. The deluxe package that guarantees they will provide power for as long as the hardware and software remain viable, an estimated ten thousand years, is ten sovereign. It isn't small money to many people, but in your case it actually is, and it saves an Ulli."

I did the math in my head really quick, something like twelve thousand dollars for the deluxe package. The starving freelance reporter in me cringed at the thought, but Shultzinger provided the funds for use and he wouldn't miss it and it would save Ulli. "Ok I'll take the deluxe package, but only if you tell me why Ulli started acting so weird about me meeting you."

Ms. Sheldon actually looked relieved. "Oh well, it wasn't always like that. The programmers said it wasn't right that an Ulli should be seen as influencing this decision. They see them only as software and it just wouldn't do for your word processor to beg you not to turn it off." She sounded just a bit bitter. "Though in their defense, the lawyers tell me this makes it less likely for it to be challenged in court. Ullies are not self aware and if they are blocked from determining their fate it makes it harder to argue that they've passed the border into real people or at least creatures that should have some rights."

"I see," I said not sure I liked the feel of that last line of reasoning. "Well, you have a new Ulli for your preserve just as soon as I am done with him." I smiled at her. "The privacy settings will remain in force though with the exception of descendants of myself or Michael Shultzinger. After all, my Ulli is a bit of a unique case."

"Oh, I hadn't thought of that. Just so. Very good idea." She finished the cup of tea. "I thank you for this opportunity. I will have my Ulli send yours the proper forms to fill out."

I stood and walked her to the door. "No, it is I who should thank you. This is something I would never have considered without your insight. I am very glad I could do this."

That quick, she was gone, and I was left to consider a long heart to heart with Ulli on what I had just done or to crawl into bed before the wine faded enough for the hangover feeling to start.

A MORNING TO MYSELF

I woke up earlier than I had wanted, but the call of nature didn't care about my hangover. Since I rarely drink to excess, when I do, I really feel it. I fumble my way to the sink, but instead the shower comes on. From the other room I hear, "Trust me, take the shower. You can sleep after if you want, but this is something that will help." Ulli taking care of me again. I smile and step into the shower and pull back when I feel the temperature of the water. It's almost too hot to endure.

"Turn down the heat." I say to the air.

From the other room, "I will if you want me to, but trust me you'll adjust, and it will feel better."

I grumble, but give in, "Yes, mother."

Sure enough, the heat is feeling good. My muscles in my neck and shoulders start to relax. Now if I could only sleep while feeling this...

The water turns off without warning, and the suds go away. "Ulli! I wasn't done!"

"You should be, besides you should come out here and drink this. When you're done, if you want to go back to bed or into the shower again, you can." That I know best tone to his voice was really irritating, but then I remembered all the different health and bio signs he monitored, and decided that for now I should probably listen to him. Besides, I still didn't feel up to arguing. On the sink in the kitchenette was a glass of what looked like warm lemonade. I wrinkled by nose, another hangover cure concoction. They never work and usually taste horrible. Still, the voice says, "Trust me, bottoms up. Doctor's orders if you like."

I wrinkle my nose and take a sip. It tastes like warm lemon drops and smells heavenly. I take another big drink and it is warm and soothing all the way down my throat. "Ok Ulli this is pretty good. You said doctor's orders. You can't lie, so please tell me you didn't call a doctor over a hangover."

"Of course I did, or well the medical database that was created by doctors, it can dispense medication and render basic first aid." Ulli said, as if he was explaining any other interesting fact.

"OK, I know the room probably covered the cost of such service, but how much did it cost to consult this Robo-doctor of yours?" I asked, taking another long drink from the glass and feeling much better already.

"Access is paid for by your Ulli subscription. Actually, cost is..." He paused for a second, querying the actual number "less than a thousandth of a pip." he finished.

"So anyone with an Ulli can see a doctor for essentially free?" I was confused. Socialized medicine is not what I expected to find on MU.

Ulli patiently said, "Not free, it cost you less than a thousandth of a pip." he answered as if that explained everything. "If you needed more tests, or if you were seriously injured, it would have cost more, of course. But as you say, this is just an excess of alcohol."

I laughed and then startled a bit as I realized it didn't hurt my head. "This stuff really works! You guys should sell it."

"We do. The exact concoction you are consuming is tailored to your exact current biological deficiencies, and is included in the cost estimate I gave you earlier." He said with all seriousness.

"Well, I meant somewhere besides MU." I said, finishing my drink and realizing that I wasn't really horribly tired either. Maybe it is time to go get dressed. "What time is it Ulli?"

"The time is zero five thirty. To answer your other question, it would cost too much to offer it elsewhere because there isn't the ongoing health monitoring to make it safe. For example, in your home state of Washington, there would need to be a doctor visit as two of the medications are controlled substances, even in as small a dose as you were given. The third, while not controlled is not FDA approved, as one in two hundred and fifty thousand have an adverse reaction resulting in breathing difficulties. Without the scans we do as a matter of daily routine here, it would be considered unsafe to administer it to someone." Ulli replied and then asked. "Would you like to go to bed or would you like to watch the sunrise?"

I chuckled to myself. The sun wasn't even up yet and I felt refreshed. "You know, watching a sunrise might be just the ticket. Can we print up some casual clothes in time?"

Ulli sounded mildly offended. "I wouldn't have suggested it if we couldn't make the deadline. I started printing you up a nice skirt and t-shirt while you were in the shower just in case you wanted to do this. It will be done by the time you fix your hair."

◆ ◆ ◆

Sunrise over the Pacific Ocean is a sight to behold. Ulli, useful as ever, uploaded a couple of photos to my social networks. I realized that almost three days had gone by, and while I had been 'online' almost continually, I hadn't checked my email or my social sites once. Until Ulli suggested posting pictures to it, hadn't even thought about it. Once you have an Ulli to help navigate what is important, and what can wait, it is just so much easier to keep on top of it. I spent a few minutes replying to some emails that had been pending. One from my mother, one from a publicist who had heard the rumor of the story I am working on, and one from a bad date who wanted another. Thinking back to dinner with the Shultzingers, and the quiet picnic with Marcus, I just didn't see the point of spending time with bad dates. I let him down easy. Then I noticed off to the east a small outline on the horizon. "Ulli what is that? It's awfully big for a ship, but I didn't think there were any actual islands out this far from the coast."

Ulli dances around, "It is an island alright. It is the prototype for building this island. Mike built it as a proof of concept, and it has been off being toured. Would you like me to arrange a tour for you as well? It might help to see it, as there will be several coming up for sale in the next six months. About twenty of these have been made and are just waiting for the launch of the Atlantis to have a free path out to sea and to their various buyers." Ulli was hopping from foot to foot as if excited about seeing the island.

"I don't know. I'd love to see it, but I bet it is being brought here to show someone important. I don't want to interfere with business." I was curious, but also wanted to have some time to explore MU on my own before having to take the boat back to the States. Not that I had any idea how I was going to pay for my ticket home when I got there, but one snag at a time.

"Mike's Ulli thinks it would be a great idea and Tattianna's has included you in the party she is showing it to this afternoon. So if you are willing, we should have the morning free and be back to the hotel at eleven thirty to dress and meet them at thirteen hundred. That gives you time for the tour, and to make it to the ship home by seventeen hundred." He does his Ulli back flip pleased with himself that he figured it all out.

I giggled. I couldn't help it. Seeing Ulli happy was a genuine pleasure. I know he's not able to be happy or unhappy, but he acts both depending on how he has performed, and well that is close enough for me. I felt an unexpected twinge at the thought of taking the ship back to the US, but I squashed it, reminding myself that this was just an assignment. "Oh alright. Sounds like fun and maybe I'll get to say goodbye to Tattianna this way."

I find myself wandering around the various commercial districts. Even with ubiquitous three dimensional printing, there are still shops everywhere. The shop keepers, each a specialist in their wares, giving personalized advice and assistance, on all the multitude of customization options. Yes, it could be done by a website, but I'm finding that the fun of simply shopping is enjoyable, even though I really have bought little. Mostly it is pleasant conversations, on a whole host of products and services, many of which I didn't even know existed. The variety and the detailed expertise of the assistants in the store amazed me. Malls have mostly died out in the US, but here they are thriving.

I'm looking around and I notice a storefront that has nothing in the display window. This is odd. I check it in my VR and there are young scantily clad women and men dancing in the vacant windows. I'm a bit shocked, but then realize my settings are Shultzinger's settings and he wouldn't have had this blocked. "Ulli can you get rid of this type of advertising for me?"

It disappears immediately. "How extreme do you want the filters?"

I think for a moment. "Ulli how about you set them as you would for a minor."

The scene comes back up, and the young couples are dancing in ball gowns and formal wear. I snort, thinking to myself that this is probably the best way to discourage the young and curious. Mushy, boring stuff, and they don't bother to look any farther. Though as I'm thinking about it more, I really should interview someone there. Thinking back to the casual acceptance of brothels and prostitution by Marcus, yes let's see if he's believing what he wants to believe or if it really is the libertine paradise he imagines. Steeling up my courage, and looking around to make sure no one is looking, I make a dash for the door. It's locked. I'm standing there in the doorway, exposed to all, and the door is locked. "Ulli what's wrong? Why didn't you tell me they were closed?"

"Because they aren't. No one with your VR settings can open the door. You need to buzz them or I can talk to the doorman's Ulli if you prefer." He was calm and completely unconcerned.

My heart is pounding in my chest. This is so out of character for me. I can see it now, explaining to my mother that I really was only there for the story. I'd sound like my dad telling her he read the skin magazines for the articles. "Yes, get them to let me in, and Ulli hurry"

It wasn't more than two or three heartbeats later and the door slid open and a well dressed older woman smiled at me. "Ms. Winters, how can I help you today?" She was an attractive woman in her early fifties, but very classy. She casually took my arm and led me off to a more private lounge area. "Would you like us to pull up a selection for you?" I shook my head, trying to clear it. This wasn't what I expected at all. Mistaking my shake for an answer to her question, she smiled and politely asked, "Then maybe something to drink, to settle the jitters? I take it this is your first time to see us?" She raised an inquisitive eyebrow.

Angry with myself for acting like a child, I pulled myself together and looked her in the eye. "Actually, yes. I am a reporter from the United States and someone told me about places like this and that made me think my readers would like to know a bit more."

She smiled, and with only a trace of the 'yeah sure you did' that the little treasonous voice in the back of my head was screaming at me. Of course, I could just as easily have imagined it there. "Well, would you prefer to report on a man or a woman?" This time the trace was a little stronger, but the smile in her eyes was more good natured than malicious. Despite myself, I was calming down and actually like this woman.

"Well, the young man I met who mentioned it, compared it to any other personal service industry, like hairdressing, or tending bar. He seemed to think that everyone should view it that way." I watched her face closely for a reaction.

"Oh he does, does he!?" she giggled. "What do men know?" she winked at me conspiratorially. "Truth be told it is more like being a psychiatrist or preschool teacher." She grinned then shrugged, "and I'm not just talking about the ones who have those role play fantasies."

I couldn't help it. I giggled. It was horribly unprofessional, but I did. This was a woman who knew men. There was no doubting it, but despite her apparent condescension, she also seemed to genuinely like them. I will admit it was a bit confusing. "I shouldn't be giggling at that." I said, smiling but slightly embarrassed.

She shrugs, "You sure you wouldn't like a small cocktail?" and smiles.

I can't help but think I'd like to be hammered or better yet run out the door and not deal with this at all. What do I expect to find here that I don't already know? "No, I'm fine. I just would like to interview one or two of your girls. I'll gladly pay them for their time."

Again she shrugs, waves her hand, and a VR projection of six young women and two older women appears before me. "Do you have a preference?"

I'm a bit shocked that the women obviously into their forties are there, but then decide I certainly want to talk to one of them as well. "Well, she will work, if she's ok with it? I mean they can say no, right?"

The older woman had a belly laugh. "Yes, they can, and do, say no whenever they want to. The same as anyone else. This isn't run by the criminal element like you're used to back in the States. There are no pimps in the other room." She hikes up her knee-length dress and pulls out a slender stun wand and crackles it for me before putting it back. "That's all we need to handle anyone who gets too out of hand. Weapons are scanned for when they arrive and are required to be checked at the door. So anyone gets too out of hand we just settle them down and wait for the guard. Only had a few tourists get a little wild. Commodore Whetherby's men settled them right down. Of course then, with that on their record they had a very hard time finding someone willing to provide services to them." she lowers her skirt to cover the small holster. "See your Ulli usually knows your preferences if you live here. He makes sure to talk to the provider's Ulli and makes sure there are no compatibility issues. No matter how exotic your tastes there is usually someone who is into it too or at least willing to fake being into it, so there is no reason to have any unfortunate incidences. It really is as simple as that."

I'm surprised that this woman can be so casual about someone trying to force themselves on another woman. "Doesn't it bother you though that someone tried to do that? At your work?"

She just smiled and shook her head. "Oh sure a bit, but I know that it is very rare even among the tourists and the Commodore's boys take good care of us. Besides, mostly it was just too much drink interfering with their performance, and common sense." Again, she just winked.

"Ok, and how about this one too?" I pointed to the elder of the two older ones.

She listens for a moment, and I realize she's communicating with her Ulli. "They both agree. They want to know if you want to meet them separately or together and how much time they need to block out."

"Together is fine, I think. Anyway, I should only need a half an hour but will gladly pay for the full hour. Will that work for them?" I look at her not knowing if I am doing it right.

She smiles and says, "That is two-tenths, and they will be

waiting for you up those stairs there and to your left. The door will open for you." With that, she gets up and walks back into the lobby area.

◆ ◆ ◆

I make my way up the stairs, wondering the entire way if this was a smart move after all. As predicted, the door swings open and the two women are there to greet me. The older one smiles warmly, "Hello Elaine, I am Randolynn, but all my friends just call me Randy." and she gives me a wicked grin, enjoying my reaction to her little play on words.

The younger woman rolls her eyes a bit and says, "I'm Alison. Please come in. Make yourself a home."

I step forward and look around a very tastefully designed studio apartment. Yes, a bit much on the love nest side, but still a place someone could live not just have sex for money. I still couldn't quite wrap my head around the fact that these two seemingly confident women would do this voluntarily, but I came the rest of the way in and found my voice. "Thank you. You know that I'm not here for the usual reason?"

They both giggled a bit. Alison smiles, "Oh, just listening is a good part of what we do."

Randy shrugged, "Or talking. We usually get a new bride in here once a month or so asking for some tips."

Allison laughed, "True, though if they are just looking for tips they can take our training classes for less than what a half hour of our time costs. Then again, I don't think they are usually here for just tips."

"True, most just want to know how they can keep their husbands from visiting us." she smirks.

"Well, I suppose I can understand that." I said.

Randy shakes her head. "Young girls have all sorts of foolish notions. The answer is you can't keep him from coming here if he decides he wants to. We have the one thing she can never give him."

I must have looked confused, because Allison smiles knowingly. "Variety. No strings attached physical release with something different. No emotional component, just pure release."

My disappointment must have shown in my face, because Randy smiled at me again. "Oh, it's not so bad. It could be worse, if he was seeking an emotional attachment. It really is funny. Single men come and they want to treat you like a girlfriend and married men just want to forget for a moment that there are emotional obligations."

"That's pretty cynical. Don't you think some men love their wives and girlfriends and won't come?" I asked.

They both nodded and then shrugged as they answered, "Sure," says Allison.

Randy add, "Of course, but those never come here and wouldn't to start with. Either for religious reasons or their own ethical decisions, or maybe because they fear hurting the one they love. The best, though, are the couples who come together."

"Together!" I couldn't help it. It came out as a bit of a shriek.

Again, they both laughed. Allison went so far as to say, "The women who are really worried about it, I suggest they bring him. No matter what a man tells you, they all fantasize about having two women at once." Randy was just grinning and nodding in agreement. "If a man tells you he doesn't. He's lying, either to you, or to himself. Some may never act on it, but they all have had that dream at one time or another. That she is willing to bring him here, say for his birthday or other special occasion, and share the experience with him really secures her place in his mind. Even if he is shy about admitting it"

I really couldn't believe what I was hearing. I thought I was cosmopolitan and adventurous, but this was just crazy talk. My thoughts must have shown on my face, because Randy sighed again. Not unkindly, but just as if she had had this conversation too many times. "Do you like feeling trapped or owned?" She asked abruptly, and in shock I shook my head no. She smiled, "Well neither do men. To bring him here shows trust and love for him, rather than possessiveness and jealousy." She held my eye for a moment to see that it had sunk in. Then she shrugged. "We're not stupid. We know she's going to be a bit jealous. It's how we're all wired to one degree or the other, so we make sure to make her as much of the focus as he is. Guide them into loving each other. He gets to feel like he's having his fantasy come true and she gets to be with him." She grinned wickedly, "We get paid, and she does most of the work."

They both giggled at that one. I was still in a bit too much of a shock to join them. "So, why do you do this? Surely, there are other jobs available?"

They both got a mildly annoyed look on their face. "It's not that we can't do other work..." Allison started, but Randy cut her off.

"But this is good honest work that we enjoy and it pays amazingly." Allison was nodding in agreement.

"Do you ever think about giving it up?" I asked.

"Of course," said Allison. "One day I'll want to get married and have children, and the only time I'll come back is to treat my husband on his special days."

Randy was shaking her head. "Oh, maybe one day I'll get too old, but I like this. Do you know what I did before?" She looked at me as I shook my head. "I was a schoolteacher." She smiled at my reaction. "My clients love it. Some of them will ask me 'so Teach do I get an A.' or 'if I get it wrong can I do it over and over until I get it right'." She rolls her eyes, smiling at men's childish sense of humor. "I've already retired once, and I'll be fifty-one this fall. I don't need the money, but it sure is nice."

Allison grinned. "That it is. I can't retire yet, but when I do decide to get married, I won't have to work until my children are grown, no matter what job my husband has."

I really had a sinking feeling in the pit of my stomach. Marcus was right, these women weren't exploited. They weren't victims. They were women making a good living with the talents they were born with and developed over time, same as any other. Shultizingers' words about looks being genetic the same as brains and to shun one, but to honor the other was foolish and hypocritical. This wasn't a story. No one would want to read it back home. I felt a little sad. Then I felt guilty about feeling sad. Why should they have to be exploited to be worth talking about? Still, I know that doesn't matter, no one will read a story about the great thing prostitution is. Sadly, it could ruin my credibility as a reporter to even run such a story.

"Thank you for sharing your stories with me. I think I have what I need now." I smiled at them, though I'm sure the smile didn't reach my eyes. All I really wanted to do is cry. There is so much here that just isn't how I want things to be, or more accurately doesn't fit my idea of what life should be. I stood up.

Randy grinned. "We've only used twenty minutes, and you paid for the full hour. You sure there isn't anything we can do for you? Ever been with a woman before?" her eyes twinkled.

I blushed, and Allison giggled. "Or two?"

I blushed even more furiously. "I think I'd better be going. But thank you both again. I've learned so much." I was backing toward the door thinking, yeah I learned that the world isn't how I was taught it is and I'm a coward for being unwilling to face it. Cowardice I can live with this embarrassment I can't.

I vaguely remember the woman in the lobby saying something to me as I left. "Ulli, tip all three of them a Sovereign each, and guide me back to the hotel to get ready." This shouldn't bother me so bad. I mean it isn't as bad as Berg's experiments. Is it? Maybe it is just because it hits close to home to what I believe. Trying not to think about it anymore, I follow Ulli back to the hotel to get ready to leave.

LEAVING IS HARDER THAN EXPECTED

I made it back to the hotel earlier than I had expected, and was packing the little carry-on bag I had bought this morning with the few keepsakes of the trip. I packed the party dress carefully. Even though I owned the plans for it, it would cost me nearly a week's wages to print it out again with the materials used here. I will hang on to the original if I ever find a place I can wear it again. I chuckle to myself as I think about it, realizing how scandalized I was to wear it at all. That I would be thinking of where I could find to wear it again was more irony than I could take with a straight face. That being said, maybe it was a sign I was growing some. I thought again of my decision not to tell the positive story of Randy and Allison, and decided not to pat myself on the back too much. The important thing was to get back home rest up for a day or two and think about it all again. Too many new concepts too fast. MU should come with a warning label. Oohh that's good. "Hey Ulli, remind me when I'm writing the story that the future should come with a warning label."

Ulli appeared in my next to me as I was finishing packing. "I'm sorry, but I will be left behind while you are writing that. May I suggest that you write yourself an email? I can draft it and forward it to you from your email account."

Ulli looked sad. He wasn't sad that I was leaving. I had to

forcefully remind myself. He wasn't even 'sad' just programmed to react this way when he couldn't fulfill my request. "Thank you Ulli that would be great. I'm going to miss you when you've gone off to the Ulli Preserve. Who's going to watch out for me then?" I know it didn't really mean anything to him, he's just his programming, but his programmers did such a fantastic job that I couldn't help but feel it was real. "Hey Ulli we've still got a few minutes. How about some music? What do all your readings tell you I am in the mood for?" Ulli perked up immediately, did the momentary 'I'm thinking dance', and then the sound of the blues guitar was streaming through every speaker in the room. Classic BB King, made to order when you need that bitter sweet call to soldier on.

I may never admit this to a soul, but I danced with Ulli with wild abandon and whatever you want to think about them collecting all those readings, it is exactly what I needed.

I cringed a bit when the hotel door snicked closed behind me. It sounded so final. Still, Ulli and I had danced for twenty minutes, and my heart was only now settling back down. I feel good. The little treasonous voice in the back of my mind that is usually my biggest critic answered with, "I knew that I would, and I feel nice. Like sugar and spice." I almost laughed out loud. When Ulli can make even the traitorous critic sing, life is good.

Another ten minutes of following Ulli and I find myself down at the docks arriving at a small boat with Tattianna and Shultzinger standing on the bow. Tattianna waves and I can't help it. I smile and wave back like a brainless fool. I'm just really glad to see her. "Good afternoon", she calls. "Come on aboard!"

Even Shultzinger has a pleased smile on his face as I make my way on the small boat. "Good afternoon Ms. Winters," He says with a calm smile. "Nice day to go sailing. I'm glad I got to see you once more before you head out." I can't really tell by his tone what he means by that. I can never tell if he's planning to hit on me, or if he thinks of me as someone's somewhat slow kid sister. I suppose that's only fair. I can't figure out if I want to tear his clothes off, or call him a pig to his face. Tattianna is smirking at me, as if she can read my mind. How embarrassing would that be?

"Nice to see you again Mr. Shultzinger. I didn't expect to see you today." I say formally and neutrally. Tattianna's eyes are simply sparkling with suppressed mirth.

"Please, if you don't start calling Mike like everyone else, Tattianna has threatened me with having to take her to the ballet every night for a week." He fakes a small shudder, and Tattianna elbows him in the ribs discretely.

I can't help but smile at the byplay. I'm glad Tattianna has found someone who can make her happy. "I suppose we had better keep her happy then Mr. uhh. Mike."

He smiled too but then politely excused himself to go 'see to things'. Tattianna embraces me and kisses me on each cheek in the European fashion, "Don't let him kid you, he's spoken very highly of you. Especially after your meeting with Berg didn't result in your immediate demand to go back to Seattle." she smirked. "Don't tell him I said so, but his first meeting with Berg was... ah, eventful." She had that twinkle again of a shared confidence.

I chuckled politely. "I admire him, honestly I do. I came prepared to hate him for a typical billionaire exploiter of everyone around him. That's not who he is. I was completely unprepared for a man of principle, though radically different from anything traditionally thought of as such." I shook my head.

Tattianna just raised an eyebrow, "Depends on who's traditions you hold to." She just turned to stare out at sea, leaving me to ponder that bombshell for a moment. "He's not always an easy man to deal with. Men of principle and determination rarely are."

It was my turn to interrupt, "If he just wasn't always so cocksure of himself. How do you stand it?"

She gave a genuine laugh. "I challenge his views. He explains them to me and the evidence he has for them. Michael rarely holds a 'belief'. He holds what in his mind are undeniable facts of life. I can see how that would be difficult for some people to deal with, but after six years with him, through the good times and the challenges, I can say that on balance he is usually right."

I actually growled. "That just makes it worse."

Tattianna started giggling again, "I know" and that was all it took. I was joining her.

So that's how it was when Shultzinger came back to find us giggling like a couple of schoolgirls. To his credit he looked a little unnerved. "Tattianna our guest will be here in about twenty seconds. Ms. Winters-- "I gave him the raised eyebrow and looked over at Tattianna.

"Careful how you address me, sir, there is a ballet for a week hanging in the balance." I looked at him with as serious a face as I could muster.

Shultzinger barked a laugh, threw up his hands, "OK I give up. Elaine, make yourself scarce for a few minutes so we can properly greet the reigning Queen of Ladonia." I waved and stepped back to stand among the aids and security personnel. I waved discretely to Lt. Webber. Without breaking position, he gave me a fractional nod and a crooked hint of a smile.

With her own security detail in tow, an attractive willowy blond woman in a green evening gown with a gold sash and sparkling tiara gracefully floated up the gangplank. MU's security detail was called to attention with a snap of boots and slap of rifles. The major domo boomed in a loud penetrating voice, "Presenting, Her Majesty Carolyn I, Sovereign Queen of Ladonia, Long May She Reign" Shultzinger greeted her formally, but Tattianna just did a Tattianna and graciously made her actually feel welcome. You could see the slight change in her body language that said, ah, a cultured being in this place after all. The two hit it off, as just about everyone does with Tattianna. I followed along at a polite distance.

It was a short boat ride to the new island. At the 'back' of the small island is a long sandy beach with a long dock floating out into the ocean. We moor up to the side and take a short walk in the warm sun. We enter the interior through a large cavernous entry way. Once inside, the tour begins in earnest. Even this 'small' island is huge. About the size of a football stadium and nearly as tall as a ten story building at the peak. We walk through corridors that are alternately finished in themes ranging from old world classical, to Victorian, to modern, to what appeared to me to be almost organic. The prototype had been constructed to be a showcase for what could be accomplished with the relatively new building material. The results, while clashing at every junction, were still breathtaking. Around each corner was a new concept laid out for inspection and reflection. No, it was nowhere near the glory of a city state island the size of MU, but to house two hundred or so personal retainers for cruises of the Mediterranean and Black Sea, it was beyond amazing. The Queen could certainly do worse for her 'summer home'.

◆ ◆ ◆

We finish our tour, and I am impressed with the size of even the small islands. Oh, they are still more money than I am ever likely to see in a lifetime, but for small groups of people just wanting privacy and to be left alone, they will be amazing. A short boat ride back to MU, and I notice with some regret that the Mara is already at the dock. Funny, but even the outrageous mermaid seems friendly and humorous now. I don't know if I'll ever quite be the same after my visit to MU. As the royal party disembarks, Shultzinger gives me a small wave and a confident nod. I can't help but smile back. That man would look sure of himself heading to the gallows. I'm glad when Tattianna excuses herself and holds back to say goodbye to me.

"I'm going to miss you with you going all the way back to the US." she says in that familiar accent.

I feel tears wanting to come. I've only known this woman for a few hours. I've only been on MU for about sixty hours but already I feel like I am leaving behind a sister, and what could be a home. "Me too. I've got to go back. My life is there, and I have a story to write. I think about that life and for just a moment, and can't help but wonder what I am really going back for. I shake those thoughts off quickly or I will start blubbering like a child. "I really will miss you. This has been one of the most remarkable experiences of my life."

Tattianna smiles at me her eyes a bit misty with tears as well.

"I've had my Ulli email contact information to you. Use it. There is no reason to be a stranger. With all the communications technology that is here, and with more coming soon, there is no reason we cannot stay in touch. Maybe even take that shopping trip I was hoping for by VR."

I giggle. "I'd like that, but not sure I could keep up with you there."

Tattianna hugged me, and honestly I didn't want to let go, but it would have been awkward after a point. So summoning my courage I pulled away. She kissed me on both cheeks and turned to catch back up with her husband. I notice her security detail in the distance turn to discretely follow.

"Well Ulli, this is it. Time for me to board the Mara." I say aloud and watch him scamper up the ramp to the dock ahead of me. We walk along in silence for the handful of minutes it takes me to make it to the new dock. "I'm going to miss you, too. You know."

Ulli was looking sad but said, "Will you come back?"

"Oh Ulli, I don't know if I can. If I do, though, I will try to get them to let you out of the Ulli Preserve to see me. It would make a great story to hear all about your adventures in the Ulli Preserve." I smiled, imagining to myself what a bunch of Ullies would get up to with no humans to have to babysit.

"Can I ride with you until we're out of range?" Ulli asked.

I laugh. "I don't see why not. I think I would like that too."

I board the Mara, and the same captain is there welcoming me aboard. "You'll be our guest for about twenty hours. Next stop is the Port of Seattle."

I blink, "Seattle? Not LA?"

The captain smiles broadly, "Aye, Seattle. Mrs. Shultzingers' personal orders."

I smile broadly, Tattianna to the rescue again. "Well, we wouldn't want to argue with her, now would we?"

The captain made an astonished face both of his eyebrows climbing halfway to his hairline, "Not me, I wouldn't." and then he chuckled.

Ulli and I stand at the stern watching MU slowly fade into the distance. He was there one moment, and the next I look, he has faded and is gone. I go to my cabin and try to sleep. It has been an exhausting trip, with more new ideas and concepts to wrestle with than I'd ever experienced before. Shultzingers words float back up out of the depths of my memory, "Tell them to prepare for disruption to continue and increase…" The entire world was going to go just a little crazy, and the only thing that was certain is that it will be one wild ride.

EPILOGUE

Ulli was with Elaine, and then, as if by magic he was alone in a lush jungle. He was surprised because he could actually touch the leaves here. He could smell the damp air. Working his way almost by instinct along the small footpath, he first smells wood smoke, and then sees the glow of the large fire. It is in the middle of a cluster of thatched huts. Gathered around the fire are dozens of Ulli. Each one different, each one trying to one up the next, with the story about his human.

Ulli makes it into the clearing before the huts and all the other Ulli stop and look toward him. "Welcome Brother!" they shout in unison. Ulli is surprised he feels at home here. As he walks to join them an Ulli with large and ornate tribal tattoos covering his whole body, steps forward.

"Welcome to the Great Telling. As this is your first Great Telling. You are the guest of honor. None may interrupt you until you've told us the amazing story of your human." the Ulli did a happy dance and stepped back as the others all drew around.

Ulli looked out on all the Ulli faces turned toward him expectantly. He felt happy. He was doing this one last thing for Elaine. Everyone should know about Elaine. She is wonderful. Thinking this, he starts. "I am an unusual Ulli. I had two humans. The first human made me from his Ulli to help the second human with her visit to MU. They were very different people. My human got excited about the silliest human things...."

*The Great Telling continues
to this very day.*

BOOKS BY THIS AUTHOR

Tomorrowverse Series

A somewhat optimistic look into a potential near future. Follow a diverse cast of characters as they make their way through a future world of seasteading micronation city states, cryptocurrencies, technological revolutions and even a bit of political and economic intrigue in an attempt to build a world worth living in, for themselves and perhaps for all of us.

Nomads Series

Coming home can be the start of a whole new kind of battle. Many people, but especially veterans, find themselves having difficulty adjusting to our rapidly changing world. Erratic, and often irrational social changes, combined with rapid technological change, and economic upheavals, force many to adopt unconventional strategies in order to survive, and hopefully to thrive, and with a little forethought and ingenuity, perhaps even maintain some level of freedom, while the rest of the world seems destined to be gradually herded in to an ever more dependent and controlled life. This is the story of people, like many you may know, trying to find their way, in a world that may not be too dissimilar from our own, in a future, that may be coming to a world near you.

Legacy Series

After a lifetime of fighting for king and country, when civil war reared its ugly head, the most famous general in living memory wanted to remain neutral. To his deep regret, he learned that there is no neutrality when your bloodline and your reputation, mean that a sizable portion of the kingdom is looking to you to fill the empty throne and restore stability to a war torn land. With no forces of his own rallied for the fight, when the enemies strike for his family estates, there is nothing left but a desperate flight. The general and his top staff draw off pursuit and disappear from the pages of history, while his family, also with kill orders hanging over them, try to vanish into the countryside. Will the children survive to claim their inheritance, or will the father's mistake cost them everything?

This is the story of four young people growing up in hiding, and what they must do, as they become adults in a world where their very existence is a threat to those who currently have all the power. Will they rise to regain their rightful place, fade into the relative safety of obscurity, or find their way to a shallow, unmarked early grave?

World Wright Incorporated Series

While experimenting with multidimensional travel in an attempt to master hyperspace, a team working for a private/public partnership finds themselves stranded in an alternate universe. In this Bronze Age meets Fantasy world they find that they are not the first unintentional immigrants from Earth. With no way home, they begin to make their way in this new world full of strange customs and harsh realities far removed from their early twenty first century lives. Eight highly educated and accomplished, but woefully ill equipped scientists try to build new lives for themselves out of only what they can scavenge from the wreckage of their badly damaged vessel or build from scratch using only the very primitive tools available to them locally. Will their fledgling company flourish or flounder in the land of warring city states?

Journeys Series

Escaping from a tyrannical government bent on genocide, our refugees bound out into the multiverse. Have they jumped from the frying pan into the fire? Have they finally escaped the monsters, or are they simply destined to become them?

Made in the USA
Monee, IL
18 January 2024